He just

"Maybe you've never lost someone in your life, Ray," she was saying. Hollis's voice was muted with feeling. "How can you possibly understand?"

Ray knew damn well what it was like to lose someone. His pain was his own private business, though. Still, it was a reflex for him to open his arms, and perhaps a reflex for her to let him envelop her in a hug.

He held his breath, wishing his body wouldn't react, since she hadn't fallen into his arms in search of physical pleasure. She was just scared out of her wits, and turning to him for consolation... even if making friends was now the very last thing on his mind.

ABOUT THE AUTHOR

With over twenty-five American Romance novels to her credit, Judith Arnold is one of the series's premier authors. Her versatility and uncanny ability to make us laugh and cry have become her hallmarks. Judith, her husband and two young sons make their home in Massachusetts.

Books by Judith Arnold

HARLEQUIN AMERICAN ROMANCE

304—TURNING TABLES
330—SURVIVORS
342—LUCKY PENNY
362—CHANGE OF LIFE
378—ONE GOOD TURN
389—A >LOVERBOY
405—SAFE HARBOR
431—TRUST ME
449—OPPOSING CAMPS
467—SWEET LIGHT
482—JUST LIKE ROMEO AND JULIET
496—OH, YOU BEAUTIFUL DOLL

HARLEQUIN SUPERROMANCE

460—RAISING THE STAKES
509—THE WOMAN DOWNSTAIRS
559—FLASHFIRE

Judith Arnold

PRIVATE LIES

Harlequin Books

TORONTO • NEW YORK • LONDON
AMSTERDAM • PARIS • SYDNEY • HAMBURG
STOCKHOLM • ATHENS • TOKYO • MILAN
MADRID • WARSAW • BUDAPEST • AUCKLAND

To Anne Stuart,
a wonderful writer and an even better friend
(although she would argue it's the other way around).

ISBN 0-373-16524-2

PRIVATE LIES

This edition published by arrangement with Harlequin Enterprises B. V.

Printed in U.S.A.

Prologue

Olivier DuChesne watched with yearning as Henri poured himself a hefty portion of bourbon, settled into the wicker armchair near the French doors and took a long sip.

At this point, Olivier saw no good reason to deprive himself of bourbon. It was too late; he was beyond saving. He might as well enjoy himself.

But Henri refused to believe his nephew was all that close to death. And he refused to ignore the instructions of the stern, starchy doctors who continued to traipse in and out of Serault Manor, clicking their tongues over Olivier's deteriorating condition and prescribing mountains of medication, the sole purpose of which was to delay the inevitable. Olivier was fifty years old and he was dying, and forgoing a stiff drink on a hot May afternoon wasn't going to make one bit of difference.

"I fail to see why you don't use that air-conditioning my sister had installed," Henri complained, gazing out through the beveled glass at the verdant garden beyond. "Those damned fans just push the hot air around."

"I don't like the air-conditioning," Olivier said, tasting his iced tea and wondering whether he could sneak a splash of bourbon into it without his uncle's noticing. "It's anachronistic. Serault Manor is more than just a residence—you know that. It's more than a hundred and fifty years old. It wasn't designed for central air."

Henri eyed the broad-bladed fan spinning futilely in the ceiling and shook his head. "Human beings weren't designed for eighty-five-degree temperatures with ninety-five percent humidity. This house is for the living, not the dead."

Olivier drank some more iced tea and grimaced, not just from its spiritless flavor but from the subject Henri had introduced. Subjects, plural. The house and death.

"I received an interesting telephone call this morning from Norville Taylor," Henri remarked with deceptive nonchalance.

At last, Olivier was going to learn the reason for his uncle's visit. He settled back in his chair and ran a finger around the collar of his limp linen shirt. His neck was damp with sweat, yet he felt a chill of anticipation.

"Norville told me he quite hates to betray a lawyer-client confidence," Henri said, his uncanny eyes bearing down on Olivier. "Nevertheless, he believes that as the last member of my generation, I ought to be apprised."

"Of what, Uncle Henri?"

"Of your effort to change a word in the legacy." Henri rotated his glass slowly in his hand, listening to the ice cubes clink, watching the muggy afternoon sunlight pass through the bourbon and turn it gold. "He told me you've asked him to alter the clause that has Serault Manor being passed down to your oldest surviving child. He said you wanted to change the word *child* to *son.*"

Olivier forced a smile. "I know what I asked him, Uncle. And I know we're living in an age of equality, feminism and such. But this is the first time since the legacy was established that the Serault heir would be one-half of a set of twins. The fact that Claire is only ten minutes older than Ollie—"

"It wouldn't matter if she were ten *seconds* older than him," Henri scolded. "You know the legacy. Serault Manor and all the land goes to the oldest surviving *child.* I didn't fuss when your mother received the estate after our father died. She was the oldest. She inherited it. You were the oldest, and you inherited it. It's been this way since the beginning, Olivier. The legacy demands it."

"I only want to protect my son," Olivier protested.

"You have a big enough estate to leave Ollie quite comfortable. He'll be well protected." Henri swallowed some bourbon, then leaned forward, resting his elbows against his knees. His blue-and-white seersucker suit had to be thirty years old, yet on Henri it looked oddly stylish. "I shouldn't have to remind you," he said, "that the legacy has existed from generation to generation for nigh as long as this house has been standing. You can't break it. Not even over a matter of twin children born ten minutes apart. The manor goes to the firstborn. It's always been that way."

Henri drained his glass, then pushed himself out of his chair. For a seventy-year-old man with several ounces of potent liquor inside him, he was surprisingly spry and steady on his feet. "I have told Norville that under no circumstances is he to alter so much as a comma in regard to the legacy. I have told him that if you make any further attempts to change the wording, I shall have you declared non compos mentis. I will not have you bringing down a curse upon your family simply because you favor your son over your daughter."

I don't favor Ollie over Claire, Olivier wanted to protest. He adored Claire. She was his princess, his darling. No father could love a daughter more.

It was because he loved her so much—her and Ollie both—that he'd tried to change the will. He wanted Serault Manor to remain in the family. *His* family. He wanted it even more than he wanted his own life.

The problem was that nettlesome phrase in the legacy: oldest surviving child. The legacy arose from a curse laid upon his ancestors one and a half centuries ago by the eldest Serault child, whose father had disinherited him in favor of a younger brother. Jean-Pierre Serault had gone to a voodoo priestess and she'd cast a spell. When Jean-Pierre's younger brother inherited the palatial *maison* and its fertile gardens, ruination had rained down upon the family. A sister went mad. A wife died in childbirth. An idiot son was born. Grandchildren sprouted boils. Not until Jean-Pierre regained title to the mansion was the curse lifted.

Thus was the legacy established. In every generation thereafter, the oldest surviving child inherited the property. To ignore the legacy was to mock the gods.

It astonished Olivier that even those dispossessed by the legacy, like his uncle Henri, strove with all their might to uphold it. And although Olivier had gone so far as to discuss altering the wording with his lawyer, he had to admit to a certain fear of what would befall his descendants if he tampered with the legacy.

Dear Lenore was a saint—only a saint would have stayed married to Olivier for twenty-five years—and he was devoted to his children. Seraults and Maraises and DuChesnes had immense wealth and power in New Orleans. They married well. They accumulated fortunes that never seemed to stop growing. Businessmen and politicians throughout the state were beholden to them.

So Olivier drank too much. His debauchery had destroyed his liver. He had lived a marvelous life, full of untold pleasure. And now that his life was nearing its end, the legacy was once again calling out, making itself felt.

Damn. He didn't want his children to suffer madness and boils. He didn't want to condemn his grandchildren yet unborn.

But to obey the legacy meant to lose the house and the land, the seat of his family's prosperity.

With melodramatic flair, he leaned back in his chair and closed his eyes. "I'm feeling tired, Uncle Henri." He sighed, touching a sallow hand to his brow. "I do believe I should get some rest."

"Indeed you should," Henri said, setting his glass on the tray and ringing for Lowery. The butler appeared at once, as if he'd been hovering just outside the solarium door, awaiting a summons. "Mr. DuChesne needs some rest," Henri instructed Lowery. "I shall show myself out."

"Very well," Lowery said, his accent a mysterious blend of upper-class British and Louisiana drawl. "I'll attend to Mr. DuChesne."

Olivier listened until he could no longer hear his uncle's footsteps on the marble tiles of the entry hall. Then he sat straighter, ignoring the twinge of pain in his abdomen. "Lowery," he whispered, "bring me some bourbon."

"The doctor says—"

"The doctor doesn't know diddly. Bring me some bourbon and then leave me be. I have to think."

Lowery nodded, filled a glass from the antique crystal decanter and handed the beverage to Olivier, who nodded his thanks and took a bracing drink. He knew Lowery would do whatever he asked.

And if he was to keep Serault Manor in his family, Olivier was going to be asking a great deal of Lowery.

Supplying a forbidden glass of booze was the least of it.

Chapter One

Ray Fargo entered the luncheonette on Vanderville's Main Street, mounted a stool at the counter and asked for a cup of coffee. The place was called Josie's, and its decor was as nondescript as its name: glass front wall, linoleum floor, pedestal trays topped by glass domes under which were displayed cakes and Danish pastries. Booths along one wall, swinging doors with porthole windows leading into the kitchen. Chrome napkin dispensers and sappy background music.

The buxom young waitress behind the counter bustled over, carrying a menu. "Would you like something with your coffee? A slice of pie?"

"No, thanks. Just the coffee is all."

She set a thick porcelain mug in front of him and filled it with coffee. "You're a long way from home, aren't you?" she asked pleasantly.

"That's right."

"I could tell by the funny way you talk."

From where he sat, she was the one who talked funny. He couldn't quite figure out what constituted an upstate New York accent. All he knew was that the folks he'd conversed with since he'd arrived at the airport in Albany last night tended to speak way too fast, and pepper their chatter with "like" and "y'know," and turn half their statements into questions.

"Where are you from?" the waitress asked, setting a plate of thimble-size creamer containers in front of him. "Somewhere down South?"

He scanned the label on one of the creamer cups to see whether the ingredients included anything of a dairy nature, then shoved the dish away. Down the counter to his left a trio of laborers in denim coveralls were chomping on doughnuts and arguing about the merits of the Yankees' relief pitching staff. Behind him, an elderly woman sat at a booth by herself, nursing a cup of tea and thumbing through the Schenectady newspaper.

"New Orleans," he told the waitress as he added a spoon of sugar to his coffee and stirred. She was talkative; it might be worth his while to cultivate her.

"Oh, wow! New Orleans! I'd love to go there. Mardi Gras and all that. And there was this movie, *The Big Easy?* With Dennis Quaid? And there was another movie, with Richard Gere and Kim What's-her-name running through the bayou in handcuffs...."

Smiling indulgently, Ray sipped the weak, brown broth that passed for coffee in these parts as the waitress rattled off every movie she'd ever seen that was set in New Orleans. "And then there was this other movie, a suspense flick with Clint Eastwood, and he's a detective? And he's raising two daughters?"

"*Tightrope,*" Ray said.

"Yeah, that's the one! And there's this scene at Mardi Gras..."

She was on a roll. He shot discreet glances at the sandwich specials posted on the wall behind the counter, at his rental car parked by a meter and visible through the diner's glass front wall, at his watch. Ten-fifteen. The day stretched ahead of him, at least eight working hours. If he got lucky, he'd accomplish what he'd come for without having to spend more than a night or two in Vanderville.

Not that a room in a motel would cost him out of pocket. This was an all-expenses-paid gig, easy money. One of the richest men in New Orleans—in the entire state of Louisiana—was paying the freight. Ray still hadn't figured out why Olivier DuChesne had chosen him, of all the P.I.'s in town, for the job. But he knew the line about gift horses. He'd take his money and thank the man, no questions asked.

"Maybe y'all could help me," he drawled when the waitress paused for breath. "I'm looking for a woman, name of Hollis Griffin. I understand she lives here in town."

"Hollis? Oh, sure," the waitress said importantly. "She's Vanderville's resident celebrity."

He'd been about to lift his mug, but the waitress's statement brought him up short. None of his information had identified Hollis Griffin as particularly famous. "A celebrity, is she?"

"Well, maybe not quite," the waitress clarified. "But she will be. She's so talented, y'know?"

According to his research, she was a photographer for a calendar publisher—not the sort of thing that would garner much publicity. "I'm a friend of a friend of hers, and I promised I'd look her up while I was in the neighborhood. I stopped by her house this morning and no one was home."

"Really? She works at her house, so she's usually there. She's got, like, this studio in her basement? Of course, she does get out sometimes. I mean, like, she's got to go hiking through the forest to collect her material, y'know?"

"My problem is, I'm kind of pressed for time," Ray explained. "If I could catch up with her today, it would make my life a whole heck of a lot easier." He leaned forward and gave the waitress his most ingratiating smile. "Perhaps if you could tell me what she looks like, I might be able to track her down."

"Well...she's beautiful," the waitress said, then sighed dreamily. "I mean, like, she's got perfect skin. Like a model on TV?"

"Is that so?"

"And black hair, jet black. And green eyes."

"She sounds pretty," he said in a bland voice. Hollis Griffin was a job. Pretty had nothing to do with it.

"She *is* pretty. My old man says she's too thin. Like, he likes a woman with flesh on her. But Hollis, she's always on the go, doing stuff, riding her bike. I guess she burns it off. Look!" The waitress pointed toward the glass wall. "There she is, right now!"

Ray spun on his stool in time to see the blur of a bicycle cruising past the window. "That's her?"

"Sure is. Everybody knows Hollis's bike. My old man calls her the Wicked Witch of the West, on account of she's always riding that bike."

"Thanks." Ray stood, dug into his pocket for his wallet and handed the waitress a five-dollar bill. "I appreciate the help."

"The coffee's only seventy-five cents—"

"Keep the change," he said, already half the distance to the door.

He hurried out to the sidewalk, shielded his eyes against the midmorning sun and searched for the bicycle. He saw it, parked on the next block.

After shoving another quarter into the parking meter next to his car, he jogged toward the abandoned bicycle. He'd already had a look around the downtown area, a few tree-lined blocks of stores and businesses charming enough to turn a man's stomach. Vanderville was the sort of cute little town where the bank that stood on the corner had a great white-faced clock built into its facade above the door, and the barbershop had a candy-cane-striped pole rotating in front of it, and the hardware store had sawdust sprinkled on the floor for decoration. It was the sort of town where one would expect to find a coffee shop named Josie's with a chatterbox waitress behind the counter.

None of which mattered. Vanderville, New York, might be a greeting-card picturesque village nestled into the wooded hills north of Albany, but Hollis Griffin called it home. That was all Ray needed to know.

He slowed to a walk, then to a halt as he studied the bike, which was chained to a lamppost in front of the post office. It had a little straw basket hooked to the handlebars, just like the Wicked Witch's bicycle in *The Wizard of Oz*.

He lifted a winged maple seed from the sidewalk, then leaned against the lamppost and twirled the seed by its stem. His gaze remained on the post-office door.

After a minute a woman appeared. She had black hair, blacker than he'd ever seen before, falling in straight precision to her shoulders. Skin as smooth and pale as bone china. Green eyes, an odd, dark green tinged with gray, like the Gulf just before a hurricane. A thin body, not skinny but slim and athletic, clothed in khaki trousers and a white blouse, with a crimson sweater draped over her shoulders and tied by its sleeves around her neck.

According to his information, she was twenty-seven years old. She looked younger, though. Like a student at some prestigious private school. Someone called Muffy, or Kitty. Or Hollis.

Seeing him loitering near her bicycle, she stopped and frowned.

Her eyes were wide, and their unusual color would catch anyone's attention. Her brows formed two thin, expressive black arcs above them. Her nose was long and straight, her cheeks sharply defined. And her mouth...

It was stunning. Luscious. A full lower lip, an exquisitely notched upper lip. Cherry red without benefit of lipstick. For a lost, silent moment, all Ray could think of was feeling those lips beneath his, molding and parting them, discovering whether they tasted as sweet as they looked.

He reminded himself of how much DuChesne was paying him and shoved his wayward lust to a dim corner of his brain. "Hollis Griffin?" he asked, courteously extending his right hand to her.

Without moving from the front step of the post office, she eyed him up and down. Her gaze lingered for a moment on his proffered hand, then rose to his face. "Do I know you?"

"My name is Ray Fargo. I'd like to talk to you, if you could spare a few minutes."

Her frown intensified. Surely his name meant nothing to her. Maybe she was contemplating his accent. Or maybe she was simply a woman of her times, suspicious of any strange man who crossed her path. He noticed the way she curved her arm protectively around her purse, hugging it to herself, as if she feared he would steal it.

"I'm a private investigator from New Orleans," he said, pulling one of his business cards from his wallet and presenting it to her. "I've come to discuss a personal matter with you."

She continued to stare at him as she took the card. After a long moment, she lowered her eyes and read the neat black print. It told her in writing what he'd just told her in words: Ray Fargo, Private Investigator, along with the Royal Street address and phone number of his office.

"Very well, then," she said primly. Her beautiful mouth scarcely moved.

"Can we talk?"

She tucked the business card into the breast pocket of her blouse. "Be my guest."

Her gesture drew his attention to her breasts. He recalled the waitress's remark about her old man's preference for women with flesh. One thing Hollis Griffin was not was fleshy.

Her proportions were perfect, though. With her lanky legs and graceful hands and her sleek, angular face, large breasts would have been all wrong. Hers was a cool, uncluttered beauty, something as pure and fresh as the bracing September breeze, the cloudless blue sky, the crisp mountain air.

"Maybe we could go somewhere, sit down and chat awhile," he suggested, tossing down the maple seed.

A flicker of apprehension passed across her face. "Chat about what?" she asked, shrinking back almost imperceptibly as he took a step closer to her.

She would likely be rattled by what he had to tell her. It wasn't the sort of thing people ought to discuss on a sun-bright sidewalk in the heart of town. "I'll answer any questions you've got, Ms. Griffin. But we really should go somewhere—"

"I'm not going anywhere with you. Not until you tell me what this is about."

"Your family," he said.

Another flicker of apprehension. "I have no family." He heard a tiny waver in her voice, so slight, only someone as skilled in picking up nuances as he was would notice.

"Let's go someplace where we can sit down," he suggested again, venturing another step closer to her.

Again she seemed to recoil. She searched the shops lining Main Street—the bakery, the hardware store, the drugstore, Josie's luncheonette. Then she faced him again, her eyes harder, more determined. "I told you, Mr. Fargo, I have no family. My parents died seven years ago."

"Your mother died." Damn. He didn't want to do this outside, in public. "Your father—"

"Died with her. In a car accident."

"Daniel Griffin was your stepfather," he said patiently. He was used to confronting people with things they'd rather not think about, rather not know. It was what he was paid to do. Most of the time, their discomfort didn't bother him. But this time, with this woman... "There's a bar across the street. I'll buy you a drink."

"It's the middle of the morning," she objected, her voice taut, her eyes bright with indignation. "And I'm not going anywhere with you. I don't even know what you're talking about." She made a move toward the bicycle, trying to elude him.

He reached out and clamped his hand around her upper arm. It was slender, the bone narrow, the muscle shaping a smooth curve beneath the cotton sleeve of her blouse.

No, he didn't like his women fleshy. Not when the alternative was a woman like Hollis Griffin.

"I'm talking about your real father," he said, then paused, watching her carefully, waiting for her to pull away from him. She returned his gaze, cool, distrustful, resentful. "You know who I'm talking about, Annabelle."

ANNABELLE.

Nobody called her that. No one had called her that in ages. The only person who had known it was her name was her mother.

And now this man.

An icy shiver skidded down her spine, and she bit her lip to keep from speaking before she had decided what to say. Ever since she'd seen the man lurking menacingly beside her bicycle—

Well, for heaven's sake, there was nothing menacing about him. He was just a man. A tall, ruggedly built man in a white T-shirt, a black blazer and evenly faded blue jeans. A viscerally attractive man with long hair the color of dark chocolate, and eyes the color of toffee, and nothing the least bit sweet in his demeanor. His face had a harshness about it. His nose was large, his jaw unyielding, his lips as unsmiling as those eerie golden-brown eyes of his. And his body, at least six feet tall and as solid as stone...

Oh, yes, he was menacing. And he was *not* just a man. He was a private investigator from New Orleans.

And he had called her Annabelle.

Another shiver racked her, extending down into her legs. She hadn't realized she was teetering until he tightened his grip on her arm, steadying her. His hand was large, strong yet curiously gentle.

"Let me buy you a drink, Ms. Griffin," he drawled.

She was too dazed to say no.

He ushered her across the street, his hand still molded to her, and they entered the Bluenose, a gloomy watering hole tucked between a vegetarian restaurant and a unisex hair salon. At night the Bluenose was a place where single people prowled for pickups, an activity that held no appeal for Hollis. She'd been there only once, dragged by her friend Sheila, and fortunately, the only thing she'd picked up was a sore throat from inhaling secondhand smoke and shouting to be heard above the high-decibel music.

In the morning, the nearly empty tavern had the shabby, dissolute air of someone who had slept in his clothes. The hanging ferns looked bedraggled, the bartender was busy wiping and stacking ashtrays, and the fellow hunched over a shot glass at the bar appeared to be asleep.

Ray Fargo led her to a booth against the wall and guided her onto the banquette. The moment he released her arm she realized that he'd been the only thing holding her up. She sank limply against the upholstery and let out a shaky breath.

The bartender moseyed over, carrying a bowl of pretzels and looking curious. "Can I get you folks something?"

"A brandy for her," Ray Fargo said. "I'll have a beer, whatever you've got on tap."

"Right away." The bartender left the pretzels and raced back to the bar, apparently delighted to have something to do.

Ray Fargo gazed across the table at her. His eyes were mesmerizing, both dark and light at the same time. She couldn't shake the feeling that they'd seen too much of life, that they saw too much of her.

Slowly, meticulously, she pulled herself together. Ever since she was a child, Hollis had been an expert at staying in control, on top of things. She was not given to falling apart, and she certainly wasn't going to fall apart simply because this private investigator had called her Annabelle.

She managed a feeble smile for the bartender as he set a snifter of brandy down in front of her and an icy mug of beer in front of Ray Fargo. Ray lifted the mug toward her in a toast, but she didn't feel like toasting anything.

She took a delicate sip of the potent liquor and shuddered as it seared her throat. "Go ahead," she said in a rusty voice. "Tell me what this is all about."

"Your birth father is a gentleman named Olivier DuChesne," he said, leaning back in his seat and regarding her with an unnervingly steady gaze. "He hired me to find you."

She closed her eyes and suppressed a grimace. Olivier DuChesne was a name she'd spent most of her life trying to forget. It was a name her mother used to whisper in despair, in hatred, in melancholy passion. It was a name that evoked antipathy in Hollis. "Why did he hire you to find me?" she asked in a deceptively calm voice.

"He wants to meet you."

"No," she said swiftly. She had absolutely no desire to meet the man who had won her mother's heart and then driven her away when she'd borne him a daughter. "I went to him," her mother had related to her so many times over the years, times Hollis had listened and times she'd wished she couldn't hear the words. "I told him that you were his flesh and blood. I said, here is your daughter. I named her Annabelle, after your mother. She's your child. She's ours."

Olivier DuChesne had rejected her. Rejected them both. "He refused to speak to me," her mother had told her. "He refused to let me into his house. He told the servants to send me away. He swore you weren't his."

So be it. Hollis was happy not to be his. "I don't want to see him," she told Ray Fargo after taking another burning sip of brandy. "He had his chance to be my father and he blew it. It's too late now."

"Well, that's the thing of it," Ray said in his soft, seductive drawl.

"What?"

"It's not too late yet, but it might be soon. Your father is dying, Ms. Griffin."

"He isn't my father," she said, sounding less certain than she had before. Not because she felt at all daughterly toward the man who had hired Ray Fargo to locate her, but because . . . because only a monster wouldn't react to the news that someone was dying. "What's wrong with him?"

"Liver disease."

She stared at her glass of brandy and grimaced. "Let me guess. He's a drunk."

"I have no idea what his vices might be. What I can tell you is that he's a very wealthy man. Very powerful. Friends in every high place there is." Ray shrugged. "I believe he's trying to right some wrongs before he dies. Abandoning you was his biggest wrong, and he wants to make it right."

"Of course," she scoffed bitterly. "He wants me to run down to New Orleans and tell him I forgive him so he can die with a clear conscience. No thanks."

"He's *very* wealthy," Ray emphasized. "I can't guarantee anything, but I suspect there's more at stake here than just atoning for his sins. Mr. DuChesne left me with the distinct impression that he wants to compensate you for whatever pain and suffering he might have caused you."

"I don't want any compensation," she retorted. The only pain Olivier DuChesne had caused her came from witnessing her mother's grief over having loved the wrong man, loved him unwisely and too well. The only suffering he'd caused her was the indignity of being fatherless, of seeking charity because her mother could scarcely support the two of them on her minimum-wage jobs. "I'm not sure what you're implying, Mr. Fargo. But I'll tell you this right now. I don't want a filthy penny from that man. He's not going to buy himself a ticket to heaven with my help."

"You're a bitter lady, aren't you?"

The accusation jolted her. How dare he accuse her of bitterness? She was tempted to toss her drink into his face, but she restrained herself. Instead, she rose to her feet, determined to get away from this man who'd had the gall to call her bitter.

With surprising speed, he reached across the table, snagged her arm and pulled her back into her seat. He flattened her hand against the table; his fingers easily encircled her wrist. His palm was warm and smooth, his grip much too strong.

After a moment, he relaxed his hold on her. She should have been able to slide her hand out from under his, but for some reason she couldn't. He didn't even have to hold her; his relentless gaze alone seemed to pin her in place.

"Don't dismiss your father so quickly," he murmured, his voice quiet but intense, as compelling as his gaze. "Give it some thought. Take your time."

"You said he was dying."

"I reckon he could fight off the Grim Reaper until you made up your mind."

"I've already made up my mind," she insisted, wincing inwardly at her faltering tone.

"Think about it, Ms. Griffin. Forget about his conscience and think about your own. Do you want to deprive a dying man of his last wish out of spite? Olivier DuChesne is your flesh and blood."

"How nice of him to remember that," she muttered, then took another swallow of her brandy and tried to pretend she wasn't acutely aware of the hard curve of Ray's palm atop her knuckles. She tried, as well, to pretend that his calling her bitter and spiteful didn't bother her, that depriving someone—anyone—of his dying wish meant nothing to her. "I can't sit here any longer," she said, glad that it was the truth. "I have things to do."

With apparent reluctance, he withdrew his hand. "What things?"

"None of your business."

He smiled. He seemed so resolute, so pitiless—and yet the smile mellowed his face, fanning creases at the corners of his eyes and etching a dimple into one cheek. When he smiled, he looked like an entirely different person, someone she could trust. Someone she could like.

"Hunting you down is very much my business," he explained, his transfiguring smile softening the words. "Now that I've tracked you down, do you think I want to let you disappear on me?"

"I don't care what you want," she said, sounding appallingly tentative.

His smile expanded. "*I* care what I want. And I care about my client. What he wants is a little thing called peace of mind, and I'd like to see that he gets it."

"He doesn't deserve it."

"Maybe he doesn't, but he needs it. And I happen to believe you're decent and generous enough to give him what he needs."

To her great irritation, she felt her lips twitching into a reluctant smile. "I think you're flattering me just to get me to change my mind."

"Darlin', if I thought flattery would do the trick, I'd be laying it on thicker than delta silt. I'd have you so buried in compliments, you wouldn't know what hit you."

The low, sonorous pull of his voice, the sensuous drawl shaping each word, was enough to erode her resistance. It was enough to make her forget the work awaiting her in her studio, the deadline five days away, the major professional step she was about to take. Her career was on the verge of shifting gears, soaring to a new elevation—and all she could think of, as she sat in the drab daytime confines of the Bluenose, was the erotic charge she felt every time Ray Fargo spoke.

Imagine if he really put that devastating drawl of his to work. His drawl, his potent honey-colored eyes, his firm lips and his stubborn chin and his big, strong body... Imagine if he mustered all his weapons against her. She'd be helpless.

"I really have to go," she said, sounding much more composed than she felt. "I have a lot of work to do."

"Taking photographs of Mother Nature?" he asked, cocking one eyebrow.

She flinched. The man knew her real name, her birth father's identity and her career. As threatened as she was by his sex appeal, she was just as troubled by his knowledge of her. "Who told you I'm a photographer?"

"I find things out," he answered with a smile. "It's my job."

She decided to fight back. "Well, if you want to know the truth, no. I'm not taking photographs today. I'm blowing up the ones I've already shot."

He gave her another breathtaking smile. "I'd love to watch."

"That won't be possible," she said laconically, then stood and slid out of the booth.

Ray quickly drained his mug and rose to his feet. He tossed some money on the table and followed her out of the bar. "I heard you were famous," he remarked, accompanying her across the street to her bicycle.

"If I were famous, Olivier DuChesne wouldn't have had to hire you to find me."

"Well, he did hire me, and I did find you."

She twisted the combination lock on her bike chain, concealing the dial with her hands as if she expected Ray Fargo to see and to memorize the numbers over her shoulder. A stupid fear—the man hadn't traveled all the way from New Orleans to steal her bicycle. Yet she couldn't shake the deep-seated fear that he was out to steal *something* from her.

Her well-being. Her emotional stability. Her very identity. He'd called her *Annabelle,* hadn't he?

"Well, now that you've found me," she said with infinitely more confidence than she felt, "I'm afraid you're going to lose me."

She noticed something hardening in his eyes, something tightening his mouth. "I'm not going to lose you, Hollis Griffin," he said, his voice as dark as his gaze.

Straddling the bike, she gripped the handlebars hard to steady her trembling hands. She pushed away from the curb and coasted down the street, pedaling for her life. She wished she could outrun his warning, could ride faster than the wind, faster than the speed of light. She wished she could escape his unsettling power, his masculine grace, his determination, the sexy undertone of his low, husky voice.

She wished she could break free of Ray Fargo. But she couldn't, and she knew it. And it frightened the hell out of her.

Chapter Two

Ray wasn't really surprised.

He watched her pedal down Main Street, her purse balanced in the handlebar basket and her shoulders square against the breeze, against the world. She was probably heading for home.

He gave himself one minute to consider going after her, then talked himself out of it. He didn't want to see her again until he'd figured out his strategy.

Given what Olivier DuChesne had told him, Ray had expected her to react negatively to the news that her father wanted to see her. After all, DuChesne had rejected his daughter, his own flesh and blood. He'd rejected his daughter's mother. Never acknowledged his offspring. Never offered his name, never mailed them a penny. Of course Hollis wanted nothing to do with him.

DuChesne himself had been prepared for such an eventuality. "I don't just want y'all to find her," he'd instructed Ray. "I want you to bring her to me. I want to see her, hold her, tell her face-to-face how very sorry I am for the way I treated her and her mother. I can't go to her, not with my health so poor. I need you to bring her to me."

Ray had made some noises, and DuChesne had quickly sweetened the deal. He would pay Ray his standard five hundred a day plus expenses, but if Ray succeeded in bringing Hollis Griffin to Serault Manor, he would receive a twenty-five thousand dollar bonus.

A man didn't offer that sort of money unless he expected the job to be difficult. DuChesne had clearly expected Hollis Griffin to be difficult.

So had Ray.

He hadn't expected her to be beautiful, though. If Olivier DuChesne had been handsome in his youth, it wasn't evident in the way he looked now. He appeared much older than his fifty years, and illness had taken its toll on him.

Hollis's mother must have been a beauty. Someone had to have contributed the genes that gave Hollis such creamy skin, such stormy eyes, such unbelievably black hair.

Seated across from her in the Bluenose, Ray had been the very model of dispassion. But alone in his car, with just the memory of her hypnotic eyes and her slim, strong body for company, he recalled the whisper softness of her voice, the way her hand had felt beneath his. He pictured her alluring, inviting, irresistibly kissable mouth. His muscles contracted and his nerves lurched to attention at the mere thought of her straddling her bike, the hard leather seat wedged between her thighs as her knees pumped, as her breath raced and the wind burned her cheeks with color.

Cool it, Fargo, he cautioned himself. She was nothing more than a job, a case, a paycheck. A woman with a whopping bounty on her head. Hell, for twenty-five thousand dollars, he'd hand-deliver a rabid possum to Serault Manor.

Just a job, he repeated to himself as he made a U-turn and cruised south to a motel on the outskirts of town where he had taken a room. Inside, he strode directly to the phone, removed from his wallet the slip of paper with DuChesne's number on it and dialed.

DuChesne's butler answered. "DuChesne residence."

Ray pulled a face. He'd met the butler on his one visit to Serault Manor, and if he'd been impressed by the guy, it hadn't been favorably. The butler had worn his affectations like a costume, and he'd spoken in a muddy British accent that irritated Ray no end.

He wasn't being paid five hundred a day to critique the household help, though. "Ray Fargo here," he said. "I'd like to speak to Mr. DuChesne."

"One moment, please."

Ray drummed his fingers on the laminated surface of the night table as he waited. At last, DuChesne's voice came on the line. "Well, Fargo? What do y'all have to say for yourself?"

"I've found her."

"Fine. Fine. When can you get her here?"

"Cut to the chase, why don't you?" Ray muttered under his breath. "If you're asking for a specific hour, Mr. DuChesne, I can't give it to you. She isn't exactly enamored of the idea of visiting you."

"Well, for God's sake, be persuasive. I'm her father."

"That seems to be a fact she'd prefer to forget."

"And New Orleans is her home."

"She doesn't see it that way," Ray pointed out. Once again he pictured her clean, fresh looks, her pale skin and preppy attire. There was nothing about her that gave any indication she had Louisiana blood in her veins. "The truth of the matter is, she doesn't have fond thoughts of you, Mr. DuChesne."

"I'm sure her mother said terrible things about me. Not that I blame the woman, given my miserly behavior toward her. I do wish to make it up to my daughter, though. Have you told her that?"

"That you wish to make up with her?"

"Make up with her, make things right with her. Make it worth her while to see me. Tell her whatever you have to, Fargo. I want that girl here."

"I'll do my best."

"Because you know what's in it for you, Fargo."

"Yes, Mr. DuChesne. I know."

"I want you to stay up there with her as long as it takes. Don't worry about the expense. I don't need you saving me any money—where I'm going, my wealth isn't going to be worth much. Spend what you have to, stay a week if you have to, but don't let her slip away."

He wanted to snap that he damned well knew how to do his job, but he refrained. "I understand."

"I need her, Fargo. Tell her I'm dying. Play on her pity. Just get her here." With that, DuChesne hung up.

Ray scowled at the dead receiver in his hand, then lowered it into the cradle. Reviewing the conversation in his mind, he shook his head.

Something was definitely odd about Olivier DuChesne. Yes, he was ill, he was desperate, but... Why hadn't he asked one single question about his daughter? Didn't he want to know what she looked like? How she wore her hair? What color her hair even was?

Letting out a long breath, Ray stood and crossed to the door. So what if DuChesne hadn't asked the obvious questions about his long-lost, just-found daughter? Confronting death had a way of twisting a man's brain and distorting his thoughts. Probably DuChesne had so much faith in Ray's ability to deliver his daughter that the old man just assumed that in the very near future he'd have his own personal opportunity to find out what she looked like.

Ray hoped he could get Hollis Griffin to her father quickly. He didn't care to hang around in this picture-perfect upstate village. He especially didn't care to spend too much time with Hollis. The longer he remained with her, the greater the temptation she posed.

He checked his watch. Nearly noon. He could drive to her house now and badger her some more, or he could have lunch first.

His grumbling stomach made his choice for him. Josie's might not offer palatable coffee, but it had a waitress with a friendly demeanor and a runaway mouth. Ray could grab a sandwich and do some research at the same time.

Pocketing the room key, he headed for his car.

HOLLIS TOOK A DEEP BREATH and let it out. She closed her eyes and counted to ten. She visualized a coral sunset, drifting clouds, gentle tides, every soothing image she could come up with.

Nothing helped. As soon as she opened her eyes, she was once again inundated with rage, panic... dread.

She didn't want to see Olivier DuChesne. She could scarcely stand to think about him. He'd caused her mother too much pain. He'd been cruel and selfish, and a lifetime of deliberate neglect couldn't be forgotten just because he was dying, just because he wanted to make amends before it was too late.

Hollis didn't want to believe her refusal to go to New Orleans had anything to do with spite.

She had a good life. She lived in a cozy house surrounded by a pine forest. She could afford to pay her bills and fill the tank of her van with gasoline. She'd had a difficult start in life, but she'd managed to make something of herself. She was about to have her first major gallery show in New York City that weekend. If she never thought about Olivier DuChesne again, that would be fine with her.

The thing of it was...

Ray Fargo.

A shudder tore through her flesh, something cold and hot at the same time. She ought to be focusing on Olivier DuChesne's abrupt decision, after so many years, to contact her. Yet somehow she couldn't help believing that DuChesne didn't pose the greatest threat to her well-being. It was that confounded detective he'd hired to find her. That cocksure fellow with his molasses drawl and his bewitching smile. That man.

It wasn't as if the intrusion of a handsome man into her life was such a traumatic thing. She'd been out with handsome men; she'd gone on several incredibly boring dates with Sheila's cousin Chet for no other reason than that he was gorgeous and she'd kept hoping his personality would improve. It hadn't, though, and she'd stopped seeing him months ago. But if another gorgeous man happened into her life, she wouldn't consider it the worst thing in the world. She wasn't looking for romance, but—

But thinking about romance in the context of Ray Fargo was absurd. He was here for one reason: to wreak havoc on her life.

So what if he was gorgeous? He was also too knowing, too aware, too capable of sabotaging her existence. The golden undertone of his eyes reminded her of a tiger's eyes, predatory and shrewd and much too powerful. The curve of his smile echoed an underlying melancholy. The sleek, hard lines of his body spoke of strength and...*prowess.* She didn't want to think about what the word implied. She didn't want to think about Ray Fargo at all.

But he was in town. He'd come for her. And she didn't have any choice but to think about him.

She left her bike inside the carport, let herself in through the kitchen door and turned the dead bolt, even though Vanderville was the sort of village where people didn't usually bother to lock their doors. As long as Ray Fargo was around, she didn't feel safe.

She pulled his business card out of her pocket, stared at it until the plain black print blurred before her eyes, then she tossed the card onto the counter. What the hell was she going to do?

Surely he knew where she lived. If he could track her down to Vanderville, he could track her down to this house.

Yet she couldn't skip town. She had too much to do before the gallery show on Saturday. She had to finish matting and framing her enlargements, get them numbered and labeled, sorted and packed into her van for the drive down to Manhattan, and make the final arrangements for the catalog that Jeff Curry was going to print for the show. Of all the times to have someone like Ray Fargo barge into her life—with news of that monster DuChesne—now had to be the worst.

She couldn't leave, yet she couldn't stay. She couldn't see Ray again until she'd gotten her nervous system under control. She never again wanted to let him make her so unhinged that she couldn't stand without his hand on her arm. She had to figure out how to fight him.

Instinctively, she descended to the basement, passed the dark room for her main workroom and lifted her Nikon from the shelf. Taking photographs wouldn't necessarily show her how to deal with the sudden upheaval in her life, but it would relax her. It would clear her mind. When she was out in the wilderness, photographing Mother Nature—

Ray's voice came back to her, that hushed, seductive velvet drawl. "Taking photographs of Mother Nature?" he'd said. She had never before thought of her art photos of mushrooms and lichens and all the other overlooked splendors of the forest as photographs of Mother Nature.

Damn the man for insinuating his way into her work, her art. Damn him to hell.

She gathered her camera, her lenses, several rolls of film and her framed backpack. She'd hike as far as she could. She would spend the daylight shooting film and the night staring at the stars, and she would pray with all her heart that after a night away, Ray Fargo's voice would no longer be whispering through her, murmuring the name she loathed with all her heart: *Annabelle.* After a night away, his eyes would no longer sear her, his accusations of her bitterness would no longer smart, his purpose for finding her would no longer tie her soul in knots.

She wished she could stay away longer than a night. She'd stay away forever, if she had any hope of ridding herself of Ray Fargo that way.

But she didn't have that hope. And all she could give herself was one night. One long, last night before he found her again.

"THERE YOU GO," said the garrulous waitress, refilling his cup and handing him a thin newspaper folded in half. "The *Vanderville Vantage.* It's our local weekly. We just got our copy delivered."

"Thanks." He wasn't sure why she'd thought he would want to read the newspaper, but he accepted it with a smile.

"Front page," she said, unfolding it for him. "I told you Hollis was a celebrity?"

"Ahh." He lowered the hamburger he'd been about to bite into and stared at the front-page article. In large block letters the headline read Local Photographer's Work In Manhattan Gallery. Below that was a two-column story, next to it what had to be the worst picture a woman with Hollis's abundant beauty could possibly take. Her eyes appeared to be two shapeless gray smudges, her nose was distorted by a shadow, her hair was disheveled and she was dressed in a baggy T-shirt that had I Like Lichens stenciled across it.

Smudges and shadows notwithstanding, she looked kind of cute.

The waitress hovered over him, so he turned his attention to the article. It was poorly written—Hollis's last name was reported to be ''Griffith'' not once but twice—but it told him more than he'd previously known about her. Apparently she was about to have a major showing of her photographs at a gallery in SoHo, opening that very Saturday evening. Five days from now.

Five days. Could he convince her to go to New Orleans before five days were up?

He continued reading the article. It described her work taking photographs for calendars that were published by a conservation organization, and her occasional free-lance work for other publications. ''I specialize in photographs of forest plants,'' she was quoted as saying. ''Mushrooms are easier to shoot than people. They don't squirm and worry about how big their noses look.''

He grinned.

''So,'' he said, lowering the paper and meeting the waitress's wide-eyed stare. ''Hollis is famous.''

''By Vanderville standards, she sure is,'' the waitress said emphatically. ''Around here, the front page is usually, like, about someone's septic system collapsing or something. Last time they did a front-page story this big about someone, it was when Hank Mullins found Satan's image in the bark of an oak tree on his property and said the tree was possessed. All the churches in town took up a collection to pay to have the tree cut down. It was weird.''

Actually, it sounded like the sort of thing that would happen in New Orleans, Ray thought with a wry smile. Only there, they wouldn't bother to cut down the tree. They'd probably hold a pagan festival and do a circle dance around the trunk.

"I wish I had talent." The waitress babbled on as Ray dug into his burger. "Jeff Curry keeps one of Hollis's moss photos in his copy center. The thing is, it takes a while to figure out it's moss. That's what's so special about her stuff, ya know? She photographs it and then, like, you don't even know what it is she's photographed. That's what makes it so artistic."

Ray nodded blandly. He had no taste for modern art—he preferred pictures where you could tell what they were just by looking at them. Evidently that wasn't the sort of artwork the so-artistic Hollis Griffin created.

He tried to tell himself that her career was as irrelevant as her large doe eyes and her ivory skin, her high breasts and her long, long legs. All that mattered was getting her on a plane with him and keeping her in her seat until the plane touched down in New Orleans, and then driving her to Serault Manor and pocketing his twenty-five thousand dollar bonus. All that mattered was getting the job done.

But he couldn't stop thinking of her taking photographs of moss and making it look like something else. He couldn't stop thinking of her at a gala in SoHo, being toasted by the highbrow art world of New York City.

He couldn't stop thinking of her parting those soft, full lips of hers around a sigh, a kiss.

He'd handled cases where it helped to know as much as he could about the people involved. With Hollis, though, the more he knew about her, the more he wanted to know. And that, he suspected, wasn't going to do him or her or Olivier DuChesne a lick of good.

He'd located her through the computer nets, starting with her birth certificate, on file in Orleans Parish. Annabelle Hollis. Mother: Moira Hollis. Father: Unknown. He'd tracked Moira Hollis through her motor vehicle records; she'd held a driver's license in New Orleans until three months after Annabelle's birth, whereupon she'd obtained a license in Atlanta. Then, Chattanooga. St. Louis. Cincinnati. Chicago. In Chicago, Moira Hollis had married Daniel Griffin. They'd moved to Albany, New York, for a few years, and then to San Jose, where after so many moves, so many addresses, Moira Hollis Griffin's license expired. So had she, along with her husband, in a head-on collision with an eighteen-wheeler.

Reaching that point, Ray had redirected his investigation from the mother to the daughter. He'd searched under Annabelle Hollis, come up empty and experimented with permutations on Annabelle, Anna, Belle, Hollis and Griffin. He'd found quite a few Anne Griffins, none of whom had the right birthday, and one Bella Hollis, an octogenarian enjoying retirement in Fort Lauderdale. Eventually the computer had spewed out Hollis Griffin, bearing a birth date identical to Annabelle Hollis's and an address in Vanderville, less than an hour north of Albany.

That was all he needed: enough to find her, enough to be certain she was truly Olivier DuChesne's daughter. Enough to bring her to New Orleans. Anything more than that and he would start thinking of her as a human being instead of a case. He'd start thinking of her as a desirable woman.

He was a professional. If there was one area in which he never let down his guard, it was his profession. If there was another, it was women.

He paid the waitress for the hamburger and the tasteless coffee, leaving her another generous tip, and asked her where he could buy a copy of the *Vanderville Vantage.* "I'd like to show it to Hollis's friend down in New Orleans," he said. It wasn't that far from the truth; Olivier DuChesne might want to see the article.

The waitress pointed across the street to a vending machine on the sidewalk outside the barbershop. "I'd give you this copy but my boss would kill me," she explained apologetically.

"I'd hate to have your death on my conscience," he said. "Take care." He felt her moony smile follow him out of the luncheonette.

He stopped at the machine to pick up a copy of the paper before climbing into his car. He still hadn't figured out his strategy. But he was good at his job. He'd think of something before he reached her house.

Revving the engine, he veered out of the parking space, driving north on the trail of his lovely, unwilling prey.

Chapter Three

She was gone.

Ray dredged up every profanity he knew—and he knew quite a few. Reciting them in the cool shadows of her empty carport didn't bring her back, however, so he stopped cursing and focused on his surroundings.

He had taken a good long look at her house when he'd driven there earlier that morning. He'd peeked into every uncurtained window and discovered that she didn't own much in the way of furniture, but what she had was clean and tidy. He'd prowled through her yard, filled with evergreens that towered over her modest brown-shingled house; he'd paced the gravel driveway and memorized the contents of her carport.

It wasn't really empty. Her bicycle was there, propped on its kickstand at the rear of the shelter, next to a wheelbarrow and shelves stacked with garden equipment and cans of motor oil. A garden hose lay coiled in a corner like a snake charmer's serpent. A waist-high stack of split logs waited for winter.

But a couple of items were missing. Most significantly, her van. That morning he'd checked out the old but apparently serviceable vehicle; its rear seat was removed and it had more than ninety thousand miles on the odometer. The lightweight pup tent she'd stowed in a drawstring vinyl bag on a shelf was also gone, as was the waterproof ground cloth she'd kept rolled up on the shelf next to the tent.

In five days the woman was going to have a gallery show of her photography, and she'd decided to go camping! Not for the joy of the outing, Ray surmised, but to get the hell away from him. Her parting words echoed in his head. *I'm afraid you're going to lose me.*

Damn it all.

He knew he could wait her out. If she didn't return to Vanderville by Saturday, he could journey to that gallery in Manhattan and corner her at the grand opening of her exhibit. But her first major art show was a special occasion, a professional milestone. He didn't want to spoil it for her by barging in and lecturing her about her sad, sick papa in New Orleans.

He scowled. It wasn't like him to place the feelings of the person he was after ahead of those of the person who had hired him. Ray wasn't working for Hollis. Whether or not he rained on her parade in New York City was irrelevant. The sad, sick papa was the one paying Ray's fee. He was the one whose feelings Ray ought to be worrying about.

The hell with her art show. The hell with her pictures of moss that didn't look like moss. He'd sit tight and wait for her to reappear, and while he was sitting tight and waiting, he'd try his damnedest not to think about those emerald eyes of hers, and that lush mouth. He'd pretend he didn't care where she was or what she was doing or how many mosquito bites she was getting while she roughed it in the wilds of New York State. He'd pretend he didn't wish she was camping out in his motel bed, instead.

Maybe he ought to have a look at that moss photo. If studying her house could give him a notion of who she was and what she was about, so could inspecting her artwork. What was the name of the shop the waitress had mentioned? A copy center. Some kind of spice, Ray recollected—chili or cayenne.

Curry, he recognized ten minutes later, when he'd returned to the downtown area and spotted the bright yellow sign reading Curry Copy Center. He parked, fed yet another coin into yet another parking meter and entered the shop.

The walls teemed with ads, flyers, business cards, samples of wedding invitations and stationery. Amid the clutter he saw what had to be the photo the waitress had been referring to. It certainly didn't look like moss. The only thing mossy about it was the color, so green it seemed alive.

He stepped closer and stared at the ten-by-twelve enlargement. Hollis must have photographed the moss from three inches away, using a fish-eye lens. It resembled dense green fibers, tufted and shadowed, the texture vivid enough to invite a touch. He didn't dare to touch it, though; the thing was supposed to be art, and he knew better than to smear his fingerprints all over it.

"Can I help you?"

He spun around. A skinny fellow in a denim apron, his gray-streaked brown hair pulled back in a ponytail and his eyes glinting amiably, approached the counter from the forest of photocopiers and other machines occupying the rear two-thirds of the store.

Ray returned the man's affable grin. "Just admiring this picture."

"Marvelous, isn't it?" The man offered his hand, and Ray shook it. "Jeff Curry," he identified himself. "What can I do for you?"

"I'm looking for the woman who took that picture," Ray said. "Hollis Griffin. I believe she's camping."

"Camping?" Jeff Curry frowned and shot a quick glance at a calendar hanging amid the jumble of papers on the nearest wall. "I've got an order to do for her in the next couple of days. I'm sure she's not camping."

"I believe she is," Ray insisted. "I'm an old friend of hers. I know the way her mind works." He shrugged and smiled innocently. "I need to catch up to her. I've got some important information to discuss with her." At Jeff Curry's hesitation, he pushed the limit. "It's about her family."

"Gee, well, if it's important..." Jeff's frown deepened, adding lines to his gaunt face. "The only place she might go would be back to the pond to take more pictures. That's where she does her best work."

"The pond," Ray said uncertainly.

"About ten miles north of town." He pulled an assortment of photocopied maps from a shelf under the counter. "It's conservation land. Real beautiful up there, and Hollis says the mushrooms are phenomenal."

"The mushrooms...?"

"You've never seen her mushroom shots? They're her trademark. They grow in the mulch along the side of the pond. Amanita. She's taken some incredible photos of them."

"That's probably where she went, then," Ray said. He shouldn't care. If she was at a pond ten miles from town, he could easily wait for her to come back.

No, he couldn't. Not easily. Not imagining her outdoors among the trees, all alone, her eyes as green as the moss fuzzing the rocks, her hair as dark as the night that would drape itself around her. He didn't want to sit in town waiting for her to come back. He wanted to be with her.

To convince her to travel to New Orleans with him, he swore to himself. To persuade her to forgive her father. That was the only reason.

He stared at the map, following Jeff Curry's roving index finger and memorizing the directions. He'd found her in Vanderville. Surely he could find her in the woods.

HE WOULD NEVER find her here.

She had left her van in the unpaved parking area at the base of the trail, and then hiked four miles deep into the forest to the pond. She knew the trail well; she'd photographed a great deal of it—the lacy lichen formations on outcroppings of granite, the delicate curl of a dry leaf, the playful flutter of a bed of ferns. She'd been photographing nature for a long time, capturing it in a way few people ever saw it. Anyone could look at a mushroom and see a mushroom. How many people could look at a mushroom and see a universe?

She wanted to share her vision with the world. She wanted to reach even people she hated, people who would never see things her way. People like Ray Fargo.

Why couldn't she stop thinking about him? The pond, the clean forest air, the cushion of pine needles on which she pitched her tent always soothed and exhilarated her. When she came to the pond to take pictures, she was able to empty her mind of everything but her surroundings: the scenery, the light, the mist that hovered above the water at dawn.

Not this time, though. She gazed at the trees bordering the pond and thought of Ray's height, his strong, sturdy posture, his immovability. She gazed at the cloudless evening sky and thought of his clear eyes. She gazed at the still, silver water and wondered if she'd looked as fearful to him as she did to herself in the pond's mirror surface.

Honestly! She had nothing to be fearful about. The man had asked her to go to New Orleans and she'd said no. And that was the end of it.

She took a few desultory photographs before conceding that she wasn't really in the mood to shoot roll after roll of film. Maybe in the morning, when the mist was with her, she'd knuckle down and get to work. Right now, all she wanted to do was watch the few yellow leaves skimming along the pond like pixie boats. She wanted to sit on a rock and remember that she was safe, that Ray Fargo couldn't get to her here, that she didn't have to do anything she didn't want to.

She leaned back against a tree trunk and closed her eyes. The honks of a V of geese winging south reached her ears from high above her. The breeze was mild, but it carried a nip of autumn in it. She heard the splash of a frog plunging into the pond by the far shore, and the snap of a twig near the trail.

Her eyes flew open at the sound of another twig snapping. Her camera equipment was stowed inside the pup tent with her sleeping bag, her propane stove and her food. If someone had come to rob her, there wasn't much she could do. If someone had come for some other reason . . .

"Idiot," she whispered to herself. She'd been wasting her time worrying about a cocky detective from New Orleans, when she could be in *real* trouble, the kind of trouble people never associated with this beautiful, remote corner of the Adirondacks.

She grabbed a rock in one hand and a stick in the other. If her aim was good enough, she might not need the stick, but she couldn't count on hitting the intruder's head squarely and knocking him out cold. She stood, flexing her fingers around her weapons, watching the mouth of the trail and praying for survival.

"Annabelle" came his soft, purring drawl as he stepped into the clearing.

She gritted her teeth and willed her hands not to throw both weapons at Ray Fargo. "Don't call me that," she muttered, staring with a combination of loathing and helplessness at his lean, hard body, his long legs and broad shoulders and ruggedly chiseled face.

Her less-than-hospitable welcome didn't seem to faze him. He continued toward her in confident strides. Evidently hiking an uneven four-mile trail in a pair of leather sneakers hadn't fazed him, either. He didn't look the least bit fatigued.

"Camping all by your lonesome doesn't seem like such a smart idea," he remarked, delivering the line as casually as if he were trying to pick her up at the Bluenose. "Y'all are mighty vulnerable out here by yourself."

Vulnerable to what? she thought angrily. No one, neither human nor beast, had ever bothered her here before. No one had hounded her the way Ray had, with the sole purpose of laying a guilt trip on her.

If that indeed was his sole purpose. Her vulnerability extended well beyond the issue of the ailing Olivier DuChesne. She and Ray were alone in the woods, miles from civilization.

She peered into his honey-brown eyes and realized he would never force her into anything, either visiting her father or... well, anything else. Ray wasn't a man who needed to rely on force. He was subtle, potent, capable of getting his way through means against which she had no idea how to defend herself.

"I'm not going to New Orleans," she declared, as if that were the only thing she was worried about.

He turned to scrutinize her pup tent, then spun back to her and grinned. "Obviously not. You're all set up to spend the night here."

"Yes. So kindly leave."

"This is public land."

"Who told you I'd be here."

He mulled over his answer and shrugged. "No one. It was just a hunch. Imagine how foolish I'd feel if I'd hiked all this way and you weren't here."

"Believe me, I wish I could have made you feel foolish."

His laughter was a dark, disturbing rumble in the surrounding silence. "I don't suppose you've got a spare sleeping bag on you."

"I don't suppose I do. You'd better leave now, before the sun sets."

He stared up at the sky, gauging the dimming evening sky. "I don't have enough light to get me back to the other end of the trail."

"And you didn't bring a flashlight, either," she guessed, pursing her lips. "Well, don't expect me to lend you mine."

His smile was less amused, more enigmatic. "I expect more of you than you expect of yourself, Hollis. Don't worry about me. I'll just spend the night."

"Not in my tent, you won't."

"Lord, no," he said in mock horror. "I'll be sleeping under the stars."

She swallowed a plaintive groan. Suddenly *she* wanted to sleep under the stars, too. She knew it wasn't wise; the ground always got too damp, and particularly at this time of year, on the cusp between summer and autumn, a bracing chill hugged the forest overnight. She'd be glad for the shelter of her tent.

But to sleep under the stars, with Ray...

"Now that we've established that you aren't going to share your flashlight or your tent," he said, "I'm probably wasting my breath asking whether you could spare me a sip or two of water. I'm afraid my canteen is back in New Orleans."

She wasn't petty enough to deny him water. With a grudging sigh, she crossed to her tent and pulled out the canteen. Ray took a few sparing sips.

Watching him drink reminded her that she was hungry. She'd packed two sandwiches—one more than she felt like eating. Sighing again, she pulled the sandwiches out of her pack and offered one to him.

His fingers brushed hers as he took it, but his eyes never left her face. His expression was unreadable—part surprise, part gratitude, but mostly something else, something that implied he knew her better than she knew herself. That bothered her. But not enough to take back the sandwich.

Without speaking, they settled on the carpet of pine needles in front of the tent and dug into their food. Hollis felt his gaze on her the entire time, and she deliberately avoided meeting it. The entire scene was too intimate, too vexing. Lord help her if he mentioned Olivier DuChesne. Lord help *him* if he did.

"Doesn't it bother your wife that you're away from home like this?" she asked when the silence began to get to her. She hoped her question would discomfit him as much as his presence discomfitted her.

With the sandwich halfway to his mouth, he paused. "I beg your pardon?"

"Here you are, a thousand miles from home, camping out in the woods with a woman you don't even know. Doesn't that bother your wife?"

He flicked a glance at his left hand, as if he expected to discover a wedding band on his naked ring finger. Then his eyes hardened on her. "I'm not married," he said, his tone colder than his gaze.

Well. She'd obviously touched a nerve, but she felt no triumph in it. "Do you travel a lot in your work?" she asked. If she was stuck with him, she might as well make the best of it. Distracting herself with polite chatter seemed preferable to thinking about how handsome he was, how isolated they were, how much she had to guard against when she was with him.

The tension ebbed from him. He leaned back against the trunk of a tree and propped his arm on one bent knee. "Not too often," he told her. "Most of my work entails punching buttons on my computer."

"I always think of detectives skulking around in trench coats and collecting clues." Damn him for looking so sexy when he smiled.

"I'm afraid I don't own a trench coat."

"How can you be a private eye if you haven't got a trench coat?" she teased, unwilling to remain stiff and wary when he was relaxed. As long as they talked this way, keeping the atmosphere light and casual, she knew intuitively that he wouldn't pressure her about New Orleans.

"According to the most recent P.I. licensing regulations, the trench coat isn't a requirement."

"Lucky for you." She polished off her sandwich, licked the crumbs from her fingers and took a swig of water from her canteen, refusing to think about the fact that his lips had touched the bottle just minutes ago. Then she passed it to him. "How did you become a private investigator? Was it something you always wanted to do?"

His tension returned for a minute. She saw his lips grow taut, his teeth clamp shut behind them. After a private struggle, he shook off whatever had gripped him. "I used to be a cop," he told her. "A police detective down in Lafayette. But I decided to quit the force and go out on my own. I like being my own boss."

"Did you like police work?"

"Not particularly."

His laconic answer should have warned her off, but she was feeling adventurous. "Why not?" she asked.

She saw his jaw working once more, his mouth tightening as he wrestled with his thoughts. In the time it took him to answer, the sun seemed to finish setting below the trees to the west. "Police work is too violent."

"Oh." Perhaps he'd seen too much violence; perhaps he'd been unable to harden himself to it. His attitude relieved her; if he didn't like violence, she was probably safe out here in the woods with him. "So, now that you're your own boss," she asked, wishing he would relax again so she'd feel even safer, "what are most of your cases about?"

"Insurance fraud."

"No kidding?" That was even more disillusioning than the news that he didn't own a trench coat.

"The insurance companies hire me to investigate false claims. Say someone falls off a ladder and sues the manufacturer for five million dollars. It's my job to find out that the plaintiff's injuries amounted to a sprained finger and a bruised shin, so the insurance company doesn't feel compelled to agree to a seven-figure settlement."

"Really?" Maybe it wasn't dramatic or glamorous, but insurance fraud sounded fascinating when Ray described it in his beguiling accent.

"I also do a lot of business with people who want me to investigate their lovers."

"You mean, catching adulterers in the act?" That sounded kind of sleazy.

Ray shook his head. "There are some P.I.'s who pay the rent by hiding in motel room closets with a camera at the ready, but that's not my kind of gig." He took another small sip of water, then capped the bottle and continued. "I'll get a woman of means who's considering marriage, and she'll hire me to make sure her intended isn't just after her money. Or to make sure he has the job he says he's got, or he isn't hiding anything from her. Women—especially women who've already been burned a few times—are mighty protective of their hearts. They don't like to trust a man unless he's been thoroughly researched."

"Just women?" she asked, intrigued. "Don't men ever ask you to check out their girlfriends?"

"Rarely," he told her. "With men, either they don't bother to trust the woman at all, or else they'd just as soon take their chances and jump in blind."

"How interesting." She sipped from the canteen, her gaze never leaving Ray. "I guess as a detective, you learn a lot about human nature."

"I'm no expert," he confessed. "I know deceptive boyfriends, and I can spot a phony insurance claim a mile away, but other than that..." He shrugged.

"What other kinds of jobs do you take?"

"Besides insurance cases and lovers?" The corners of his mouth twitched up into a mild smile. "Missing people."

"I'm not missing!" she protested, surprising herself with her vehemence. When she thought of missing people, she thought of kidnapped children, runaway teenagers, bail jumpers, embezzlers hiding in Bimini—not someone like herself, who had always lived well within the limits of the law and never tried to hide from anyone.

"As far as your father was concerned, you were," Ray pointed out.

Hollis could have retorted that her father had been the one missing—by choice, he'd been missing from her life. But she didn't want to get into an argument with Ray. The most important thing was to make sure he didn't use this as the start of a new campaign to get her to visit her father.

"When you find a missing person," she asked, doing her best to keep her tone level, "do you always go chasing across the country after her?"

He shook his head. "Usually I provide the client with the information he wants and let him make contact himself. I think your father wanted me to talk to you because he figured you wouldn't talk to him."

"He got that one right," she said, grumbling.

"And he couldn't come to Vanderville himself. He's too sick to make such a trip. As I understand it, he rarely ventures out of his house."

Hollis experienced a twinge of sympathy. She didn't want to feel sorry for Olivier DuChesne, but she couldn't help herself. "He's a prisoner in his own house?"

"As prisons go, his is pretty grand."

"What do you mean?"

He gazed at her from beneath lowered lids. "Olivier DuChesne lives in a mansion smack-dab in the middle of the Garden District. You'd never even know it's there. It's set back behind other houses on several acres of prime real estate. From the road, all you can see is a wrought-iron double gate set in a six-foot-high stone wall, with a little video camera attached to it, so his butler can identify visitors before admitting them."

"It sounds like the CIA."

He smiled. "If you pass muster, the gates swing open and you drive up a long brick driveway. At the end stands a mansion, three stories high, all brick and stone, with pillars and verandas and balconies and such. Four chimneys, Palladian windows, marble stairs leading to the front door. It's as big as a small castle, and it's worth a fortune. It's called Serault Manor."

"Serault Manor? What's Serault?"

"I believe Serault is a who, not a what. The first owner, probably. I don't know the history of the place. But it does have a history, I'm sure of that."

"Is it old?"

Ray nodded. "Well tended, though. The gardens alone must require an army to maintain. I was there only once, when your father signed me on. I don't know much about antiques and decorating, but when I walked inside, the place surely reeked of money. Old money."

"Great. I'm the bastard child of a dynasty," she said, appalled to hear the asperity in her tone. Ray had accused her yesterday of being bitter, and although she had never before thought of herself as a bitter person, something about Olivier DuChesne brought out the worst in her.

"It doesn't have to be that way," Ray reminded her gently. "Your father wants to acknowledge you as his daughter."

"Bully for him." She bit her lip to keep from sounding off before she got her temper under control. "I really don't want to talk about him."

Ray's smile expanded. The sky had faded to a deep blue, filtering shadows across his face and making his eyes seem even brighter in comparison. "Fine," he drawled, an edge of teasing in his voice. "Let's talk about you instead."

She stifled the urge to say no. If Ray realized how defensive he made her feel, he might use that knowledge against her in some way. "What about me?" she asked with deceptive poise.

"Why in the world does a person decide to make a career out of taking pictures of mushrooms?"

She let out a breath. Talking about her work was easier than talking about her father. "Mushrooms can be beautiful."

"They can be poisonous."

She nodded and gestured toward the amanita that sprouted along the edge of the pond. "Those over there are. Some people say they'll give you a psychedelic high, but they're a nasty little fungus. They photograph well, though."

"I saw a photo of yours over at Curry Copy. If no one had told me it was moss, I would never have guessed."

Curry Copy, she thought. Jeff Curry was an old friend; he must have figured out where she was spending the night, and shared his guess with Ray. Hollis wondered how Ray had tracked down Jeff. No doubt his job as a detective involved talents he hadn't mentioned when he'd described his work to her.

"The photograph of the moss was so enlarged and distorted, it didn't even look like what it was," he said.

"It looked exactly like what it is," she argued. "It's just that most people don't think to look at moss or mushrooms or lichens the way I do."

"What made you decide to photograph these things?"

The sky grew darker yet. From deep in the woods came the mournful cooing of an owl. Because the dark fell gradually, her eyes were able to adjust. She could see Ray as clearly now as she could a half hour ago.

Maybe even more clearly. Since he'd arrived at her campsite, she'd gotten to know him better, somehow. She'd stopped worrying that he would overwhelm her, either with his physical strength or with his powers of persuasion.

"I stumbled into it by accident," she told him. "I had an after-school job in high school, working at one of those storefront developing places. You know, photos in an hour."

"Real arty stuff they do there," he joked.

She concurred with a grin. "The manager did studio portraits, and he sold camera equipment. I learned bits and pieces—just enough so I could do the job. Anyway, I started college, and then my parents died. My mother and stepfather," she clarified, then grimaced. She'd thought of Dan Griffin as her father for years, even went so far as to take his last name as her own. Why, all of a sudden, was she thinking of him as her stepfather?

She knew why. The reason was sitting less than six feet from her.

She smothered the reflexive grief that threatened her whenever she thought of the accident that had left her an orphan. "You're a detective," she said softly. "You know all about their dying."

"I know enough."

"I couldn't stay in school. Even if I could have afforded to, I was hardly in the mood to sit in a classroom taking notes on *Madame Bovary* when what little family I had had just been wiped out."

"Of course not."

"So I returned to the photo lab. I worked full-time, overtime, volunteering for any extra work that came up. Eventually, my boss started letting me help him with his studio portraits, and in time I got pretty good at it."

"Studio portraits are a far cry from the lower plant forms."

"Studio portraits," she said, "are usually of screaming babies, whining children, or adults who picture themselves a heck of a lot better-looking than they actually are, and they blame you when their photos come out looking like them instead of like Michelle Pfeiffer or Mel Gibson. Mushrooms may be poisonous, but they don't squirm and they don't talk back."

"When you put it like that, they sound like the ideal house pet."

"And you don't need a litter box." She laughed, aware of how absurd she must sound, waxing affectionate over mushrooms. "I didn't do any plant photography in San Jose. But after I'd settled my parents' affairs, I decided to leave town. There were too many memories."

"What brought you to Vanderville?"

"I had an old friend living in the area. My family lived in Albany for a while, and after we left, Sheila and I stayed in touch. When I told her I was at loose ends, she urged me to move here. I thought I'd only stay a short while, till I figured out where I belonged. But I liked it here. I needed some time to myself, and Vanderville is small and safe, and there are forests and mountains just waiting to be photographed."

"Forests and mountains and fungus."

"And ferns and lichens."

He regarded her thoughtfully. In the diminished light, he seemed almost a silhouette, all dark, sharp angles. Night hemmed them in on all sides, shrinking the clearing and drawing deeper shadows from the surrounding woods. Hollis wondered if Ray was as acutely conscious of their solitude as she was—and if so, whether it filled him with both apprehension and expectation, doubt and trust.

"You aren't really going to spend the night here, are you?" she asked, her voice a husky whisper in the still air.

"You aren't really going to send me back down that trail in the pitch dark, are you?" he countered, his voice as husky as hers.

If she sent him back down the trail, he'd probably fall and hurt himself, or get lost. The trail took too many twists and turns, and it was booby-trapped with outcroppings of stone and uncovered roots just waiting to trip hikers.

But to have Ray here, alone with her in the woods, breathing the silvery moonlight air... "Well, you can't sleep outside the tent. You haven't got a sleeping bag. You'll freeze to death."

He smiled slyly. "That would make you happy, wouldn't it?"

"As much as I resent you, Fargo, I don't want you to die."

"We're making progress." He stood and dusted off the seat of his jeans, then gripped her wrists with his hands and hauled her to her feet. "Let me stay in your tent, Hollis. I promise I won't touch you."

He was touching her now, his fingers encircling her narrow wrists, warm and firm, sending a tremulous warmth up her arms. His gaze was touching her, and his serious smile. His nearness was touching her, tripping switches in her soul, making her far too aware of how long it had been since she'd last let a man touch her.

"I'll hold you to that promise," she murmured, forcing herself to meet his gaze with hers.

Time passed, no more than a second or two, but it felt like forever. Then he released her hands and nudged her toward the tent. "Better wash up before it's too dark to see," he said.

It was already too dark. The world seemed too dark when Ray was with her. Dark with mystery, dark with need, dark with the possibility of danger. Dark with the understanding that she'd been alone too long, and that Ray Fargo was the wrong person to lead her away from her loneliness.

She reached into her tent and grabbed her flashlight, desperate for its light.

THE TENT WOULDN'T have been too small for Ray and another man to share. Maybe even Ray and another woman. But for Ray and Hollis...

It was much, much too small.

She was snugly zippered into her sleeping bag; he lay on his side, his back to her, as if that would give her more privacy. Although she didn't move he knew she wasn't asleep. Her breathing was too shallow. Her body was too still.

His presence made her uneasy. That would have been fine if he'd been trying to keep her unbalanced in an effort to lure her to New Orleans. But the fact was, her presence made him just as uneasy. He felt her body warmth fill the prism-shaped shelter; he inhaled her sweet, clean fragrance. If he shifted an inch, his spine would press up against her.

He wanted to shift that inch more than he could remember wanting anything in a long time.

"Y'all wouldn't happen to know any ghost stories, would you?" he asked, more for his own benefit than for hers. If he didn't fall asleep tonight, he'd be useless tomorrow. And if he didn't unwind, he was never going to fall asleep. A good bedtime story on any subject other than Hollis might help.

He heard a faint laugh behind him, and took that as an invitation to roll over. She lay on her side facing him, and he found himself staring into her wide eyes. She was so close. Close enough that her breath whispered across his cheek.

He inched back, anxious to put as much space between them as possible. If he felt her breath on his face one more time, he'd have to feel it on his lips, in that charged, magic instant before his mouth took hers.

"I don't know any ghost stories," she said.

He took a deep breath and held it until the muscles in his abdomen unclenched. "It seems strange camping out without a ghost story," he remarked in a deceptively even voice.

"Is that some voodoo New Orleans custom?"

He chuckled. "No, darlin', we aren't all into voodoo—though I do have a neighbor who might know some witchcraft." He pictured Nanny Carre, the elderly woman whose batture house stood a hundred yards down the levee from his. To an outsider, the tiny village of shacks on the batture might seem like some cult retreat, if not one step removed from camping. Ray's tiny, rickety cabin on the edge of the Mississippi, where he went whenever he needed to escape the city's hurly-burly, was held together by hard work and hope, not voodoo. Closing his eyes, he pictured the shack swaying on its piles, the gas lamps and wood stove that lit the place and kept it warm, the rudimentary hoses that brought water into the sink. True, it had a roof—one that required frequent patching—and a floor, but Hollis's tent probably had as much structural integrity.

He loved the batture house, though. Loved patching the roof and shoring up the piles, loved fleeing the city and burying himself in the fog that swelled up from the river.

Hollis would probably love it, too.

That was an odd thought, and he shoved it out of his mind. "Ghost stories are from when I was a kid," he explained. "My brother and I would camp in the woods behind our house all the time in the summer. My dad gave us some old tarpaulins from his boat, and we'd string one up in the trees above us and spread one out below us and smack the skeeters from our skin all night long. Tommy would steal some food from the pantry, something real nutritious, like potato chips, and we'd pig out and give our folks a chance to—" He cut himself off.

"To what?"

She'd asked; he might as well answer. "To enjoy themselves in private. We had a small house, and the walls weren't exactly soundproof."

"Well." Far from shocked, she sounded amused. The moonlight filtering through the mesh caught on the curve of her cheek as she smiled. "Wasn't that thoughtful of you."

"Tommy and I were such good boys," he said with false modesty.

"Was this in New Orleans?"

He laughed. "New Orleans is a big city. There aren't too many places where a couple of kids with an oily tarp and a bag of potato chips can camp out. No, I grew up down south, in Terrebonne Parish. Bayou country. My mama's folks were Cajun. My father's people came from Galveston."

"And your father had a boat?"

"He's a shrimper. Tommy works the boat with him, now. There wasn't enough work for two sons—which was okay with me. I don't think I'd have cared to spend my life hauling shrimp."

"Your family sounds nice," she said wistfully.

Nice wouldn't have been the word he'd use to describe his family. His mother had a temper hotter than Tabasco sauce. His father grew sullen when the shrimp weren't running. Whenever Ray journeyed down to

Dulac, Tommy's wife would collar him and whine about how Tommy spent too many evenings hanging out with the other shrimpers, drinking bourbon and talking shop. They were always running short of cash; Ray was always sending them a little something.

As families went, the Fargos were far from perfect. But even an imperfect family was better than nothing.

Hollis had nothing. DuChesne didn't count as family.

"It's just a thought," Ray said, "but if you saw DuChesne, you'd have a family. You'd have *someone.*"

"Ray." Her smile vanished. Her tone turned icy. "Don't push me, or I'll kick you out of here so fast—"

"I promised I wouldn't touch you. I didn't promise I'd stop talking."

"Maybe you ought to make that promise right now. I didn't ask you here, Ray. I don't want you here. So shut up."

He wanted to shut her up. With a kiss. Her mouth was still too close to his. All he had to do was lean over, rise above her, press her down under him, and...

And that would be breaking a promise. Ray's scruples weren't bothering him, but he had to preserve what little trust Hollis gave him. If he lost that, he'd lose her for good. He'd never change her mind about her father.

In truth, though, he wasn't thinking about DuChesne right now. He wasn't thinking about the job he was hired to do or the bounty he hoped to collect.

Rather, he was thinking of Hollis herself. He was thinking about how alone she was in the world. "Everyone needs a family," he observed. "Everyone needs someone—"

"I already have someone." Her tone was low but intense. "I have my mother."

"She's gone, Hollis."

"I have memories."

"You could have more."

"Memories are all I need," she said, then abruptly rolled over to face the side wall of the tent, pulling her sleeping bag protectively around her.

She needed more than memories. He knew it, and she knew it, too. He'd heard the anger in her voice, the hurt, the sorrow. She was all alone in this world, a brave, beautiful, lonely woman, and she needed something more.

For one brief, irrational moment, Ray believed he would have traded his soul for the chance to give her what she needed. If it wasn't her father, her inheritance, her proper place in the DuChesne family, then whatever it was, he would give it to her.

But the moment passed, and the night grew still around him. And he realized how very little he had to give to a woman like Hollis.

Chapter Four

He slept poorly. There were plenty of reasons: the cold, the lack of proper bedding, the lumpy ground under him, the creaking of trees and the rustling of leaves as the wind sifted through the surrounding foliage.

Hollis. Her nearness, and her inviolability.

Ray wasn't a soft touch when it came to women. He liked them, he got along with them, but for their own good he didn't let them get too close. He knew too much about loving and losing, and he didn't take chances, either with them or with himself.

Nothing about Hollis invited him to take a chance. Nothing about her indicated that she harbored even remotely friendly feelings toward him. Yet lying beside her throughout a night of chilly winds and hooting owls, certain that if his arm accidentally brushed her shoulder he would be unable to keep from pulling her to himself and pressing his body to hers, and . . .

Cripes. He had to deliver her to New Orleans, collect his money and get on with his life. He didn't need to be feeling all these things for Hollis Griffin.

Sometime before dawn, he'd drifted into a dreamless slumber. The abrupt sensation that he was alone awakened him with a start. The air in the tent seemed to have dropped in temperature; his body twitched with a shiver.

The screened triangle in front of him let in the milky light of early morning. Squinting at his watch, he read that it was six-fifteen.

Still shivering, he sat up and stared for a minute at Hollis's unoccupied sleeping bag. How could she have gotten away without rousing him? If he had lost her again... Well, he'd just have to find her again. And once he did, he'd hog-tie her and haul her bodily back to New Orleans. Then he'd get his twenty-five thousand dollars and hit the road.

He rolled his shoulders to loosen them. Outside the tent, he laced his sneakers, then stood and chafed his arms with his hands, trying to rub the early-morning chill out of his muscles. Great curls of white mist wafted up from the silver-smooth surface of the pond, lending the scene a surreal aura.

But Hollis was very real. When he saw her lying prone alongside a log near the edge of the pond, braced on her elbows with her hands cradling a camera, he felt a relief much more profound than his frustration at the possibility that she'd eluded him. His shivering stopped.

He stared at her across the clearing. She was a sleek figure, poised and intent, oblivious to everything except the small garden of mushrooms at which her camera was aimed. As Ray gazed at her, what he saw wasn't so much her striking coloring or her graceful beauty but her concentration, her sense of purpose.

If sleeping in the tent with her had turned him on, watching her work, noting the soft, glossy drop of her hair to her shoulders, the sharp line of her jaw, the slender curves of her body, the inherent grace in her wrists and hands as she wielded her camera...

It turned him on all over again, even more than before.

He lowered himself to sit on an outcropping of granite. From his vantage he could see not only her but the vapor-shrouded pond, the dark green spires of the evergreens, the pink opalescence of the early-morning sky. His forearms sprouted goose bumps in the cool air, and he considered getting his jacket from inside the tent. But that would necessitate leaving the rock and his glorious view of Hollis in her element, doing her thing.

She continued to shoot pictures of the mushrooms for a while, then hunkered down on the far end of the log to shoot more pictures from a different angle. If she'd glanced up she would have seen Ray. But she was too absorbed with her camera work to notice him.

He ought to be equally absorbed with his own work: convincing her to come with him to New Orleans. If taking pictures of fungus was her job, delivering her to Olivier DuChesne was Ray's job. Yet for a few precious minutes, while she was too wrapped up in her photography to notice, he had the opportunity to ogle her, and he wasn't going to waste it.

God, but she was beautiful. Just watching the adroit angling of her wrists, the quick fluttering of her fingers... He wondered how her fingers would feel fluttering across him. He wondered what it would be like to have a woman like her concentrating on him the way she concentrated on her mushrooms.

She stopped tapping the shutter button, stretched languidly and spotted Ray observing her from his perch on the boulder. Frozen in midstretch, she stopped smiling. Without a word, she stood, fitted the lens cap onto her camera and left the pond, moving in long strides that drew his attention to her legs. The hell with her hands; he wanted to feel her legs on him, around him.

No he didn't. He wanted to be immune to her.

Before she reached him, he turned and headed back to the tent to get his jacket. She joined him there, kneeling on the ground cloth and tucking her camera carefully into its case. Her shoulder bumped his and he smothered a groan. She smelled of the woods, pine and clean mountain air. Her hair looked almost blue-black in the eerie dawn light.

Cool it, he ordered himself. *Start a conversation. Pretend this is a morning just like any other.*

An absurd notion. To be alone in a forest with a woman like Hollis hardly constituted a typical morning. "Did you get any good pictures?" he asked, annoyed by the inanity of the question but unable to come up with anything better.

She shrugged. "I don't know. The light was interesting." Her voice had an edge to it, a roughness, as if she were as tightly strung as he was.

"It looks like a pretty fancy camera."

"It is." She stuffed the case into her backpack, then got very busy rolling her sleeping bag.

"I'm impressed you can even think about work at this hour, without any caffeine in your bloodstream."

"If you hadn't drunk my water last night, I'd have enough to make coffee."

He lifted the canteen and discovered it half-full. "Fire up your stove," he suggested. "There's enough in here for at least one cup."

She pursed her lips, as if irritated that he would dare to contradict her. Tugging the canteen out of his hands, she scowled. There was no way she could disagree with him; there was definitely a good cup of water left.

Refusing to look at him, she set up her propane stove and inserted a fuel cartridge. Then she poured the water from the canteen into a mess-kit pot and set it on the burner to heat. As graceful as she'd been when she'd been taking pictures by the pond, now she moved jerkily, doing her best to avoid banging shoulders with him a second time.

"Anything I can do?" He'd meant the question in terms of the coffee and the tent, but when she spun around and glowered at him, her eyes blazed with rage.

"You can back off," she snapped.

Determined not to meet anger with anger, he counted to five before responding. "I wasn't aware I was on."

"I wish you weren't here, okay? I came to the woods to get away from you."

"You're not going to get away from me, Hollis. So you might as well save yourself the effort of trying."

She turned and stared at the pot, as if her only goal in life was to disprove the old saw about watched pots never boiling.

It occurred to him that if she honestly hated him, he'd never get her to go to New Orleans to meet with DuChesne. He had to make it as easy as possible for her to trust him. "Look," he said, edging closer to her, "I'm sorry about last night."

"What do you have to be sorry about?" she asked archly.

"Barging in on y'all. I know I was about as welcome as the flu. Maybe if you stopped thinking of me as your enemy—"

"Don't flatter yourself, Fargo. I don't think of you as my enemy."

"Then stop thinking of your father as your enemy."

"Olivier DuChesne is a monster. You're just a nuisance." The water in the pot had reached a rolling boil, and she pulled a couple of envelopes of instant coffee and two plastic cups from her pack. Ray wasn't sure he could stomach instant coffee—around these parts, even the genuine brewed coffee was nothing to brag about—but her willingness to share her sparse supplies with him told him more than all her verbal sniping. He'd drink what she gave him and issue not a word of complaint.

She emptied a packet of coffee into one cup, then filled it half-full with water. Even at double strength the beverage tasted watery to him. "One of these days," he said, doing his best to strike up a friendly chat, "you're going to have to try New Orleans coffee."

She shot him a quick, skeptical look.

"They French-roast the beans, then mix in some chicory before brewing. It's got a serious flavor. Puts hair on your chest."

"That's just what I need," she muttered. "A hairy chest."

Much as he would have enjoyed discussing her chest with her, he thought it better to concentrate on eroding her distrust. "Admit it, Hollis—I haven't tried to pressure you into anything, not going to New Orleans or anything else."

She peered over the rim of her cup at him. "Am I supposed to thank you?"

He sighed. "Just give me a fair hearing."

"I've heard everything you have to say."

"I'm not going to coerce you, Hollis. I only think that, once you consider it, you'll realize going to New Orleans is the right thing to do."

"The *right* thing? What makes my paying my respects to that SOB the *right* thing?"

Ray studied her in the increasing light. Pale sunshine glimmered on the surface of the pond and caught in the gossamer curls of her lashes. "He needs you."

"Oh. He needs me. Where was he when I needed him?" she fumed, anger causing the tendons in her neck to stand out. "Where was he when my mother and I were broke? Where was he when my classmates asked me who my daddy was? I needed him then, Fargo, and he wasn't there for me."

"Fair is fair, I reckon," he drawled. "Do unto others as they've done unto you."

Fury simmered in her eyes the way the water had simmered in the pot on the stove. If only, like the stove, she had a valve he could twist to lower the heat.

If only he could convince himself her anger was directed at her father, not at him.

"I'm not out for revenge," she said, obviously struggling to keep her tone level. "I don't want to do unto him as he did unto me. I just want him to leave me alone."

"He left you alone for the past twenty-seven years, Hollis. And from the sound of things, you're not all that pleased about it."

"Why should I be pleased? I was the one who got labeled a bastard, but he's the real bastard. He never cared anything for me. He never did a single damned thing for me. Why should I do anything for him?"

"There's that bitterness again, darlin'. Wouldn't you be better off if you got rid of that? Just chuck it. Let go of it."

"If I want to be psychoanalyzed, I'll go to a shrink," she snapped, hostility dripping from each syllable. "I sure as hell won't turn to you for counseling."

He gamely sipped some coffee and mulled over his options. If she wanted to play this thing in the upper registers, he could easily match her in sarcasm, rage and withering condescension. But he wanted to keep the discussion civil and respectful. He knew that if she only stopped raging—against her father, against him, against the restless night they'd spent just inches away from each other—he could reason with her. "I don't want to fight with you, Hollis."

"Then you shouldn't have mentioned New Orleans."

"Why don't you like being called Annabelle?" he asked.

Her eyes flashed a bright green. He hadn't realized until that moment that she could get any angrier. "I thought you didn't want to fight with me."

"I didn't know saying Annabelle would lead to a fight." Her seething silence told him she wasn't going to explain why she hated the name she'd been given at birth. "I'll tell you what," he said. "You tell me which subjects are taboo, and I'll do my best to avoid them. So far we've got New Orleans, your father, your name—"

Abruptly she lurched to her feet and stalked away. He polished off his coffee, allowing himself a small grimace at its metallic taste, then rose and followed her to the edge of the pond. She stood facing the water, her arms hugged to herself, allowing him no entry. It took every ounce of his willpower to keep him from sidling up behind her and wrapping his arms around her. Willpower, plus the comprehension that if he did wrap his arms around her, making friends with her would be the last thing on his mind.

"I'm sorry," he said.

His apology seemed to thaw her slightly. She turned and peered up at him, and he saw the storm in her eyes, a clash of light and shadow. "Your showing up here unexpectedly, with news of that man . . . I don't think you understand how difficult this is for me," she said slowly, her voice muted but thick with feeling.

"Maybe I don't." That was a lie. Of course he understood how difficult it was for her. He'd had to convey far worse news to clients in the past, news that a long-lost relative was in fact dead, news that a beloved beau was in fact a con man. But for Hollis's sake he could pretend the news that her father had decided to acknowledge her existence was the most devastating revelation he'd ever been paid to make.

"I have no mother, no father..." She faltered, her voice crowded by a sob. She turned her gaze back to the pristine pond and paused until she'd pulled herself together. "Maybe you've never lost anyone in your life, Ray. How can you possibly understand?"

He clamped his mouth shut to keep from explaining to her, in the most brutal of terms, that he knew damned well what it was like to lose someone, and he'd as soon throw her into the pond as listen to her patronizing him, addressing him as if he had no idea what pain was all about.

His pain was his own private business, though, and he kept it inside, safe, away from the light. "You're right, Hollis," he said coldly. "You're the expert when it comes to loss. Nobody in the world has ever suffered as much as you have."

She glanced up at him again, her expression strange, as if she were actually seeing him for the first time. "I didn't mean it that way," she apologized, then averted her gaze again. "This hasn't been easy for me, Fargo. I don't know how to deal with any of it. My father, the memories... You."

It was a reflex for him to open his arms, and perhaps a reflex for her to step into them, to let him envelop her in a hug. She felt surprisingly delicate in his embrace, almost fragile, her shoulders narrower than he'd expected, her waist slimmer. Her hips brushed lightly against his and he held his breath, praying for his body not to react. She hadn't fallen into his arms in search of physical pleasure. She was scared out of her wits, and she was turning to him for consolation. That was all he could give her.

She rested her cheek shyly against his shoulder. A few strands of her hair snagged on the overnight growth of beard stubbling his chin. "Don't take it so hard, darlin'," he murmured. "Things will work themselves out."

"I don't want you holding me," she murmured, the words muffled by his shirt as she nestled her face against him. But she made no move to back away.

He made no move to let go of her. Tangling his fingers into her hair, he urged her head down onto his shoulder. She trembled—whether from pain or anger or arousal, he couldn't tell.

Holding her didn't arouse him the way he'd thought it would; it aroused deeper instincts, a need to comfort that he hadn't experienced in a long time. Her rancorous accusations were forgotten. He wanted to comfort her, to make everything better.

She remained within his embrace for a moment longer, then let out a tiny sigh and backed away. Her cheeks were slightly damp, and that tempting lower lip of hers, while quivering, curved upward in a reluctant half smile. "Maybe I'll forgive you for all this someday," she muttered.

"Maybe you will," he said, unable to return her smile.

SHE LIFTED the last sheet of proofs from their final bath and hung them to dry. The tang of chemicals in the air burned her nostrils, and she peeled off her rubber gloves and slipped out of the room, eager to breathe fresh air. In a while she would know for sure what she had, and whether it would be good enough.

That was, in terms of the photos she'd taken that morning. As far as her own life went, she knew what she had, and she knew it wasn't good enough. And she blamed Ray Fargo for making her acknowledge that truth.

They had parted ways at the parking area at the start of the trail a couple of hours ago. Ray had driven off, and she had gone home and headed directly downstairs to her cellar darkroom to develop her film. She wanted to think about the amanita she'd shot that morning, the arrangement of her prints for the catalog, the upcoming show. She wanted to think about anything but what she couldn't stop thinking about: Ray Fargo, goading her, then consoling her, enraging her so much she'd had to flee from him, and then gathering her to himself and sheltering her from her own fury.

Just before he'd taken her in his arms, she'd seen in his eyes a pain to match hers, a torment deep inside him. And when he'd closed his arms around her, she'd wondered who was leaning on whom, who was taking comfort and who was giving it.

Damn. She didn't need this complication right now. She didn't need to be thinking about men or the lack of them in her life. She didn't need to be thinking about how utterly wonderful it had been to have the powerful contours of a man's body against hers, the tender roughness of a man's whiskered chin against her forehead, the possessiveness of a man's arms circling her. She didn't need to be feeling this hollow, throbbing hunger inside her.

Definitely not now. And definitely not when the man with the powerful body and the chin and the possessive arms was Ray Fargo, a representative of that beast down in New Orleans.

Sleeping with him in her tent last night had been torture. Even snug inside her sleeping bag, she'd been much too conscious of Ray beside her, his legs parallel to hers, his breath mingling with hers. Every time he'd shifted, she'd pictured him in her mind—his athletic legs, his tapered chest, the sleek muscles of his arms. The only garments he'd removed before retiring had been his sneakers, yet she'd pictured him... She blushed just to remember her overheated dreams of his blunt-tipped fingers skimming over her skin, the unruly brown waves of his hair spilling over his face as he hovered above her, the mystifying golden light in his eyes communicating want and need and passion, and then his body following, expressing that want and need and passion even more vividly.

Where had her erotic visions come from? Her, or him, or the two of them combining in some way to create a dangerous chemistry?

She shook her head. The fantasy was hers alone. Ray Fargo didn't want her or need her. His only passion was to do the job he'd come to Vanderville to do: get her to see Olivier DuChesne before the man died. Get her to journey to New Orleans and absolve her father of every sin he'd ever committed against her.

That was the only thing Ray wanted from her. And it was one thing he'd never get.

"YOU WENT CAMPING with her?" Olivier DuChesne inquired, sounding dubious. "How very quaint."

Ray sat slouched in an upholstered vinyl armchair in his motel room, his feet propped up on the bed and his gaze riveted to the parking lot visible beyond the window.

Because he'd been out in the woods, he hadn't been able to telephone DuChesne with an update last night. Apparently DuChesne had telephoned him, instead. Ray had arrived back at the motel to find a message waiting for him.

He could have phoned DuChesne as soon as he'd reached his room, but he hadn't. He'd told himself he needed to get some breakfast into his body before he talked shop with the man who had hired him. He'd driven to the small grocery store off Main Street, bought an orange and some crullers, along with a jumbo cup of take-out coffee, and carried his food back to the motel room. After eating, he'd taken a long shower. Then he'd gone to the motel office and purchased a copy of the Albany daily paper from a machine. He'd read it from beginning to end, then returned to the grocery store for a couple of beers and a bag of pretzels.

He wasn't sure why he was procrastinating. DuChesne was his client, the man with the checkbook. And no matter how much Hollis resisted, Ray remained convinced that reuniting her with her father would be a good thing.

Yet after spending the night in the woods with her, he felt disloyal talking to DuChesne. That one embrace by the water's edge had done something to Ray. If taking Hollis in his arms had been just a sexual experience, he wouldn't have been so unnerved by it. But it hadn't been just sexual. It had been something much more complex, much harder to define. He'd wanted Hollis in a way that transcended the physical.

He'd been shaken by it. And now he felt funny going behind her back to scheme with the father she didn't want to know.

"If she wants to go camping," DuChesne remarked, "she can camp out among the gardens here. I want her at Serault Manor, Fargo. When are y'all going to bring her to me?"

"I can't very well abduct her," Ray said patiently. "And let's face it, Mr. DuChesne, if you want to make things up with her, she's going to have to come to you of her own free will."

"Well, break her will if you've got to. I want her here."

Ray frowned. Breaking a person's will—especially someone with a will as strong and fierce as Hollis Griffin's—wasn't his style. He much preferred to *bend* a person's will, to reshape it. "I understand why you're impatient, Mr. DuChesne, but believe me, forcing her isn't going to solve anything."

"The hell with solving things, Fargo. This isn't a mystery. It's a stubborn girl who needs to come see her father."

No, Ray wanted to argue. DuChesne was the one with a need to see Hollis.

What was the worst possible outcome? Ray would fail to bring Hollis to New Orleans. She would live the remainder of her life as bitter as she'd lived the first part of it. DuChesne would go to his grave with a heavy conscience. But life didn't come with a guarantee that all loose ends would be tied up before the Grim Reaper came to call. If DuChesne passed away before he was able to resolve his relationship with his daughter, it wouldn't be Ray's fault, would it?

"I'm doing the best I can," he insisted. "Have you spoken to your priest?"

"About what?" DuChesne flared, exhibiting more spirit than Ray expected. "What's he got to do with it? I'm not dead yet."

"I didn't mean it was time for last rites," Ray explained. "I meant, perhaps you could unload some of your guilt—"

"What guilt? I haven't done anything to be guilty of!"

Ray's frown deepened. What was this all about, if not DuChesne's attempt to cleanse his soul of guilt? "You abandoned Hollis and her mother."

"Oh, that. Right. I have to apologize to Hollis. In person. No priest is going to be able to help me with that."

"Well, as I said, I can't force her to do anything. I want her to make the choice to come to you. If I force her, it won't work out."

"There's nothing to work out," DuChesne grumbled. "I'll do whatever apologizing the situation requires—but you've got to bring her here first."

"I'm trying, Mr. DuChesne. If you'd rather send someone else up here to finish what I've begun—"

"No," DuChesne said, and Ray let out a sigh of relief. He didn't want someone else to take his place in Vanderville—and when he thought about it, he realized it wasn't just because he wanted to reap the bounty DuChesne was offering for his daughter's return.

Ray had to stay for Hollis's sake. It was one thing to twist her arm, another to let her be strong-armed. He had to stay here to make sure the thing was done right and she chose to accept her father, freely and from the goodness of her heart. "Trust me, Mr. DuChesne," he said. "I'll get the job done."

"I'm sure you will. I had you checked out. You've got a reputation for achieving results."

Ray smiled wryly. As someone who checked out other people for a living, he couldn't very well object to being checked out himself. A man with DuChesne's wealth and power could have hired any P.I. in Louisiana for this job. He had to have chosen Ray for a reason, and Ray was self-assured enough to assume the reason was that he was damned good at what he did.

"But please, Fargo—whatever it takes, just get her here. My time on this earth is growing short. I need to have her here with me before it's too late."

"I understand."

"Bring her to me. I'll take care of the rest."

"Okay."

Ray lowered the phone into its cradle and took a long swig of beer. Reviewing the conversation in his head, he felt inexplicably uneasy. Once again DuChesne hadn't asked a single question about Hollis herself, what she was like, how she lived. He hadn't even asked why she and Ray had gone camping last night. Ray wondered if he even cared.

If he didn't care, why was he so eager to meet her? *Bring her to me. I'll take care of the rest.*

Although Ray hadn't checked DuChesne out as thoroughly as DuChesne had apparently checked him out, he knew a few things about the man. DuChesne had been married for some twenty-five years; his wife, Lenore, sat on the boards of several charitable societies. DuChesne himself was a member of some of the oldest, if not the most respected, clubs. He personally funded one krewe's Mardi Gras float every year. He held banking interests, and he owned rental properties, an industrial park near the airport and that remarkable estate in the middle of town. His wife's family had been plantation people up in St. James; she'd come to the marriage with her own money.

Ray hadn't had to dig deep to find out any of this. It got trotted out in the society pages all the time: Lenore DuChesne presiding at a masque ball to raise money for the cancer wing at this or that hospital; Lenore DuChesne dressed in antebellum finery at a Battle of New Orleans memorial celebration; Lenore DuChesne presenting a check to the aquarium.

He wondered how Lenore DuChesne, queen of New Orleans society, had taken to the news that her husband had sired an illegitimate daughter twenty-seven years ago. He wondered how DuChesne had explained Hollis's existence to his family. "I have an illegitimate daughter, and I'm paying a detective a small fortune to get her down here so you can all welcome her into your hearts before I'm gone."

Not exactly a charming scene. But it wasn't Ray's concern. All he had to do was bring Hollis to DuChesne.

The dying man's voice echoed inside Ray's skull. A clear enough statement, a simple mandate. *Bring her to me. I'll take care of the rest.*

Why did those words leave him colder than he'd felt during his long night in the woods?

Chapter Five

"You know," he drawled, "I think I'm beginning to see it."

He had appeared on her doorstep two hours ago, carrying a bulging paper bag containing a thick sirloin steak, a couple of baking potatoes, a bag of juicy vine-ripened tomatoes, each the size of a softball, a head of lettuce and a six-pack of beer. "I was afraid," he'd said, "that if I called ahead and asked you out for dinner, you'd turn me down."

"I would have," she'd confirmed. The peal of her doorbell had summoned her from her basement workroom, where she'd been trying to decide which prints to include in the catalog. Her jaunt to the pond yesterday had deprived her of precious time needed to get the final details ready for her show, and it had failed to protect her from Ray. Now she faced tons of work—and the man she seemed unable to avoid.

"So I brought dinner instead," he'd told her, giving her a winsome, utterly irresistible smile and extending the food-filled sack.

She'd accepted the inevitable and let him in. "I won't be eating for hours," she'd warned. "I'm working."

"If I help you, will it go faster?"

It would. It did. They'd spent those hours in her workroom, and though Hollis would never admit it, his assistance had proven invaluable. Dozens of prints had to be matted and framed, numbered and cataloged. Ray had stacked the framed prints, helped her arrange the unframed ones, ignored her when she muttered to herself and jumped to attention when she asked him to bring her the straight edge or another assembled frame.

Every now and then she would catch him frozen, staring at a close-up of a fern or a pinecone enlarged so many times it resembled a mound of weathered shingles. He would study the photograph, his brow furrowed, his eyes luminous. Then, sensing her gaze on him, he would smile sheepishly and shift back into gear.

He'd spoken not one word about New Orleans, not a single whisper about Olivier DuChesne. Not a hint of the reason behind his presence in her life.

Because they'd accomplished more than she'd expected, she permitted herself the pleasure of a leisurely dinner. She couldn't recall the last time she'd eaten such a filling, well-balanced meal, or enjoyed it so much. She leaned back in her chair, feeling stuffed and content, and studied the man across the table from her.

While they'd been working in the basement, she hadn't allowed herself to think about the embrace he'd given her that morning, the unwanted warmth it had brought her, the unwanted yearnings it had kindled inside her. Now, though, Ray had reverted to being a man again—a tall, virile man with a sexy smile and solid shoulders, capable hands and a body that could pack away a huge steak and all the fixings and show nothing for it but lean, hard muscle.

"What do you mean, you're beginning to see it?" she asked, hoping she wasn't giving him an opening to resume harassing her about her father.

He lifted his nearly empty glass of beer, but his eyes remained on her as he finished off his drink. "Your pictures," he said.

"Oh?"

"They're strange, Hollis. You can't deny that. But I can see how people might call them artistic when you blow them up so they look more like abstract shapes. When I first thought about it, I thought the idea was nuts. But now I get it."

She returned his grin. "I'm relieved to know you don't think it's nuts anymore."

"What your photographs do is make people pay attention to things they might not have noticed otherwise. There's a real beauty in those pictures, even if it does kind of creep up on a person," Ray said. "I'm betting your show on Saturday is going to be a huge success."

His flattery embarrassed her. "Is this what you mean by laying it on thicker than delta silt?"

"All I'm saying is, you're a talented lady, Hollis."

"Enough!" She could feel her cheeks burning with a blush. A quick sip of beer cooled her down. "I'm not so talented. The truth is, when it comes to art, success is usually a matter of doing something new.

Nobody's done art photos of the sort of thing I do art photos of. It's a novelty."

"You're too modest."

"I'm realistic. If the show in New York is a flop, I won't be surprised."

"I will." He drained his glass, then set it on the table and pushed back his chair so he could stretch his legs. "What all do you still have to do before Saturday?"

"I have to get the catalogs for the show printed. Then I have to truck everything down to New York, get the prints hung at the gallery, take a deep breath . . . and then guzzle champagne at the opening-night party."

"They're throwing you a party?"

"They're throwing my *show* a party," she explained. "It helps to build excitement for the exhibit. Reporters and art connoisseurs are supposed to come and consume all the champagne, and then—if I'm lucky—they'll spread the word that it's a show worth seeing."

Ray nodded. He appeared genuinely fascinated.

Maybe it was all an act; maybe he was feigning respect for her career as a way of softening her up. Maybe she had lost her ability to read people. But she honestly believed Ray cared about her work—and about her.

If she was wrong about him, if he was merely a master of deception, tricking her into thinking he was interested in her life so she would agree to whatever he wanted . . . Well, he was destined to fail. Because she had no intention of agreeing to anything.

She surveyed the table, the empty dinner plates and the bowl of leftover salad. "After a meal like this, I feel like I should whip out a homemade cheesecake for dessert. I'm afraid the best I can do is a package of store-bought cookies."

"No need for dessert," he told her. "I'm pretty full."

"How about a brandy?"

"No, thanks."

"Another beer?"

He shook his head and nudged his empty glass away. "I've had enough."

He wasn't much of a drinker. She'd seen him enjoy a beer on a couple of occasions, but never anything stronger. Tonight he'd brought a full six-pack, but he'd made one single bottle last the entire meal.

"What?" he asked, evidently reading her bemusement in her face.

She shrugged. "I don't know. I watched lots of Humphrey Bogart movies when I was a kid. And I've read a few Dashiell Hammett novels. I thought detectives were heavy drinkers."

"Just the ones with the trench coats," he joked, although his expression remained enigmatic.

"You don't smoke, either."

"I'm a regular angel, aren't I?"

She grinned at his sardonic tone. "Seriously, Ray. I know, it's none of my business, but...I mean, is there a reason you don't drink more than a single beer at a sitting?"

His eyes glowed with an intensity she had trouble confronting. He traced his index finger around the rim of his empty glass, his sharp gaze remaining on her.

"Yes," he said finally. "There's a reason. And you're right. It's none of your business."

She was too curious to let him discourage her. "Do you have a problem with hard liquor?"

"No."

"Then why—"

"I don't like the taste of it."

He continued to trace the rim of his glass, moving his finger in circle after circle after circle. A muscle in his jaw worked overtime, pulsing with tension. She lifted her gaze to his eyes once more, mesmerized by their golden light, by the inscrutable emotion behind them.

At long last he spoke. "There was a time in my life when I was living in some pain, and I tried everything—including liquor—to numb myself. Now the taste of liquor reminds me of that time."

"Oh." How much more could she ask? How reckless could she be? "You seem like a stable person. I can't imagine you getting lost in a bottle."

"Circumstances sometimes put us in places we can't imagine," he said cryptically.

"What circumstances?"

He could have bolted. Could have pushed away from the table and made his departure. Could have told her once more that it was none of her damned business.

"I lost my wife," he said.

She sighed sympathetically. "Divorces can be a nasty business."

"It wasn't a divorce."

"Oh." She frowned for a moment, and then understanding dawned. "Oh, God. She died?"

"Yes."

"Oh, Ray—I'm so sorry." Her words struck her as pathetically inadequate. As someone who'd lost what little family she'd had, Hollis could guess at the anguish he must have suffered. *I'm so sorry* barely scratched the surface.

She remembered the flash of fury she'd seen in his eyes that morning at the pond, when she'd accused him of never having lost anyone. To lose a parent was terrible, but to lose a wife, a lover, a partner...

"I'm sorry," she said again. Not only for his loss but for having been so insensitive that morning, so wrapped up in her own misery.

"Yes, well...so am I."

"I could see how something like that might drive a person to drink."

"Yes."

She was full of questions now, overflowing with them. Yet she refused to give voice to them. Ray had obviously told her more than he'd wished.

Rising from the table, she gathered a few plates and carried them to the sink. She needed to focus on something other than the man in her kitchen, the stark sorrow she felt emanating from him.

She reassured herself that if he'd truly resented her questions, he would have left. But he chose to stay, joining her at the sink with a couple of plates. "Would you like me to dry?" he asked as she filled the basin with warm water and detergent.

"You don't have to."

"I know I don't have to." He plucked the dish towel from the hook above the sink, then pulled her hands out of the sudsy water and dried them off. "Don't get all mopey on me, Hollis."

"I'm not getting mopey," she said, aware that her vision was clouded with tears. Aware that even after setting aside the towel, Ray didn't seem in any hurry to let go of her hands. "I just... I feel like an idiot," she said. "I shouldn't have lit into you the way I did this morning, when I implied that you couldn't possibly understand how I felt."

The smile he gave her was slow and dark, stirring her nerve endings and making her breath lodge in her throat. "Don't feel like an idiot."

At that moment, she didn't. She felt like a woman, alone in her home with a man. A man whose large, hard hands enveloped her small, slender ones, and whose beautiful light-and-dark eyes refused to release her from their penetrating gaze, and whose tall, strong body was close to hers, so close, so unbearably close.

She knew he would kiss her an instant before he did. Yet there was no way to prepare herself for the subtle, searing pressure of his lips on hers, or for the fierce desire that seized her as his mouth moved against hers and his fingers tightened around her hands, or for the deep, dazzling pleasure she felt standing in the shadow of his body, their lips brushing, sliding, touching in a dance of barely restrained passion.

She wanted to kiss him forever. She wanted to take his tongue in her mouth, and wrap her arms around him, and merge her body with his. She wanted to kiss him until his pain and hers was vanquished, until nothing existed beyond this room, this moment, this man. She wanted to kiss him until the hot tension in her belly spread throughout her entire body, igniting her everywhere, igniting him.

She had never wanted anything as much as she wanted Ray Fargo.

The man Olivier DuChesne had hired to find her.

She lowered her head and he drew back, although his hands remained around hers, his thumbs sliding back and forth across her knuckles. His breath sounded much more even than hers. Apparently this kiss hadn't affected him nearly as strongly as it had affected her.

"This isn't a good idea," she said, wanting to trust him, knowing she shouldn't.

"You're right."

She stared at his feet, shod in his familiar leather sneakers, a fraction of an inch from her own feet. If she leaned forward the slightest bit, her hips would press into his, her breasts would collide with his chest and she would kiss him again, and again, until all her self-protective reflexes were silenced, all her doubts banished.

It was a bad idea, they both agreed. "I guess— It's just— We've been spending all this time together, and—"

"Hollis." Still clasping her hands, he lowered his arms and pulled her gently against himself. Once again she was leaning on him. Once again it felt too good.

"I mean—you're far from home, and I'm all keyed up about the show this weekend, and—"

"Hollis." At last he released her hands, but only to wrap his arms loosely around her. "Relax. Your show's going to be fine. And I'm not homesick for anything but a good cup of coffee. We're attracted to each other, that's all."

His blunt assessment coaxed a smile from her. "You make it sound simple."

"It is simple. Of course, if we act on that attraction, it's going to stop being simple real fast."

"Then I guess we'd better not." She wondered why such a logical conclusion made her so sad.

With obvious reluctance, he let go of her and picked up the dish towel. "Now, then. Y'all wash, and I'll dry."

Forcing a smile, she glanced up at him. He was smiling, too. His smile looked just as forced.

And his eyes looked just as sad.

HE WONDERED WHY he'd told her about his wife.

Not that he'd told her much. But it wasn't a subject he discussed with anyone. Even his family knew better than to mention it. The tragedy of his wife's death was a wound that would never completely heal, and anyone who knew Ray knew better than to reopen it.

Yet with Hollis, he'd not only answered questions she'd had no right asking, but then he'd gone and kissed her. Exactly the thing he'd wanted to do since the moment he'd laid eyes on her. Exactly the thing he should never have done.

Because now that he'd kissed her once, he wanted to kiss her again.

Her lips had felt softer than they'd looked, sweet and pliant, and her sigh had told him everything he'd needed to know about her feelings. Her hands, curling and squeezing his, and the hushed, nearly soundless moan that escaped her, and the way her body had molded to his when he'd pulled her into his arms, had told him.

But, as she'd said, it was a bad idea.

They were back in her cellar, in a brightly lit room with an enlarger against the far wall and a table running almost the entire length of the room. She had a score of five-by-seven prints scattered across the table. She was trying to put them in some sort of final order for the catalog. "I couldn't have gotten so much done without you earlier," she'd said. "If you want to stick around, I'd be grateful."

Ray had nothing to offer in the way of suggestions, but it was an invitation he couldn't resist.

He observed the light, quick grace of her hands as she slid the photos around, murmuring to herself as much as to him—"I can't have two lichen shots on facing pages. It looks so redundant"—and glancing up at him for confirmation. When called upon, he did his best to nod earnestly, while his mind wandered to a memory of her velvety lips on his, the timid pressure of her mouth, the silken warmth of her breath mingling with his.

"What do you think?" Hollis asked, blessedly pulling him out of his provocative ruminations. "Does this fern shot look good juxtaposed with that one?"

He managed a smile. "I'm no expert, Hollis."

"That's why I'm asking you."

"Then, sure. They look good together."

She smiled. "Okay. They'll go side by side. Tell me, Ray—is my father married?"

It took him a minute to recover from her sudden switch to a new topic. Another several seconds to register that she hadn't referred to Olivier DuChesne as a creep or a bastard or any of her other angry epithets, but simply as "my father."

"Yes," he answered, wondering whether that answer would please or distress her.

She gave nothing away. Her complexion, so delectably flushed after he had kissed her, retained its usual ivory tone as his answer sank in. Her expression was guarded. "Does he have children?"

"Besides you? A son and a daughter. Twins, I believe."

"Twins!" Her eyes brightened to a luminous silvery jade, and her mouth, the mouth with which he'd so recently developed an intimate acquaintance, spread in a smile of unabashed delight. "I have a brother and a sister?"

"Indeed you do."

"Wow." A dazed laugh escaped her, and she shook her head, as if astonished by her own reaction. "Of course, they aren't *really* my sister and brother."

"Half sister. Half brother."

"No—I mean, family, Ray—real family. It's ridiculous for me to consider a bunch of strangers my family."

The pensiveness in her voice touched something inside him. She was depriving herself of the family she obviously wanted, for no better reason than that old resentment and bitterness. "They can become your family," he pointed out. "Not in an instant, but given time, you could build a relationship with them. I don't rightly know much about Olivier DuChesne's children. I believe they finished college fairly recently. But your father's wife gets her name in the local news a fair amount. Half the charities in town stay afloat thanks to her efforts. She funds hospital wings and cuts ribbons on a regular basis."

"She sounds busy."

"Busy doing good works."

"Probably to compensate for her husband's sins."

Ray might have reproached her for her negativity, but he only laughed. "Probably."

"What irony," she muttered, her gaze fixed on a series of prints but her thoughts quite clearly on her father. She rearranged the photographs and shook her head. "DuChesne's wife raises money for good causes, and meanwhile, her own husband's child grew up with nothing. If my mother and I had remained in New Orleans, maybe Mrs. DuChesne could have made us her favorite charity."

"Were you and your mother a charity case?" he asked. It was a tactless question, but Hollis had already ventured well beyond the limits of tact with him. He saw no reason to exercise restraint with her.

She scowled. "If welfare's the same thing as charity, then yes, we were." She nudged the photos into a particular arrangement, then jotted herself a note and set them aside. "Before my mother had me, she'd been a waitress. Her parents were scandalized when she became pregnant. They didn't want anything to do with her. Neither did my father, as you know."

He couldn't miss the bite of her words. But she kept going before he could speak in DuChesne's defense—which was just as well, because until he'd hired Ray to find Hollis, DuChesne's behavior regarding her had been indefensible.

"My mother took jobs whenever she could. But when I was young, there weren't many child-care options available, so we wound up on public assistance. When I started school, she got work waitressing, but the money was never anything we could count on. Sometimes we lived in public housing. Sometimes we accepted handouts from the local food banks. I doubt the DuChesne twins had a childhood like mine."

He pictured a recent photo of Lenore DuChesne in the newspapers, dressed in an elegant suit, with elegant jewelry adorning her wrists and earlobes. A woman like that would not have had to feed her children handouts from a local food bank. "No," he murmured. "I reckon your sister and brother had everything they needed. But that doesn't mean—"

"Don't worry, Ray," Hollis said briskly. "I'm not jealous of them. I had what I had. They had what they had. The fact that they had more than I did isn't their fault."

"Still, no one would blame you for envying them."

"I don't. I had my mother, whose good work was to accept me and love me and raise me the best she could, with no help from anybody."

"It's too bad her parents didn't help out."

Hollis stacked a group of photos with a crisp efficiency that Ray found oddly disturbing. "Well, she and I had each other. And she loved me. And we had friends, and eventually we had Dan Griffin. My stepfather was a good man, Ray."

Unlike her real father, he filled in.

She seemed busy with her prints, tapping them into a neat pile, setting them down, lifting them and tapping them neater. "Dan Griffin didn't adopt you, did he?" Ray asked. He knew the answer, but he wanted to keep the conversation going.

"It wasn't necessary. He treated me well and he loved my mother. I didn't need the formalities."

"But you took his last name."

"Because my mother did, and I wanted the same last name as she had." Hollis's hands were nearly flying. Her eyes darted, drifted, refused to settle on Ray.

"Family is more than a name, Hollis. It's more than having the same last name as your mother. I know you want to have a family again—and you can. That's exactly what Olivier DuChesne wants for you."

"What he wants is a clean bill of moral health. I don't care how many good works his wife has done—"

"Your face lit up when I mentioned the twins, Hollis. I saw it. You *want* that family."

"Don't tell me you're going to psychoanalyze me again," she snapped, slamming down the stack of photographs and giving him a long, hard stare. "I had a family. My mother and Dan. No, he didn't live in a mansion in the Garden District, and no, my mother didn't host charity balls. They couldn't afford new cars, so we bought them used. They couldn't afford prime rib, so we lived on macaroni and cheese. They couldn't save a dollar, couldn't remember a doctor's appointment, couldn't remember what day the rent was due. So I took care of the bills and the appointments. But it was worth it, just to know I had them and they loved me."

"You seem to have turned out all right, considering," Ray remarked. His voice was bland but his mind churned, trying to take in everything she'd told him. He had grown up in a household of little means, his comfort dependent on whether the shrimp were running, his future predicated on the seaworthiness of his father's boat. But despite the unpredictable fortunes of the Gulf and the spicy tempers of his parents, Ray had grown up knowing who he was and where he belonged.

That Hollis hadn't known that kind of security as a child explained a lot, not least of all the strain of bitterness that occasionally surfaced in her. "Maybe," he ventured, "some of your anger at your father ought to be aimed at the way society treats people whose families don't fit the traditional ideal. Especially twenty years ago. People weren't so open-minded about single mothers then."

"This has nothing to do with *people,* Fargo. It has to do with Olivier DuChesne. If he'd made an honest woman of my mother, I would have had a normal childhood."

"Who can say your mother and DuChesne wouldn't have been a terrible match?"

"If they had been, they could have gotten a divorce. It still would have been better than nothing. And I'll tell you this, Ray—" she waved a finger at him, no longer bothering to pretend her mind was on her photographs "—if Olivier DuChesne had done the right thing by my mother, she would have knocked herself out to be a good wife for him. She loved him. Even after he did her dirt, she loved him. She used to cry, not because he'd turned his back on her and me but because he didn't love her the way she loved him. To her dying day, I think she still loved him." Hollis glanced at another photograph, then set it down and lifted her gaze to meet Ray's across the table. "My mother had her faults. But she had a lot of love inside her. And she was always very proud to call me her daughter."

Unlike DuChesne. The unspoken accusation hung in the air. "Perhaps it was your father's misfortune that he didn't marry her."

She curled her lip. "My mother wouldn't have been any good at cutting ribbons and funding hospital wings. I'm sure my father got what he was looking for when he married the charitable Mrs. DuChesne."

Ray should have pushed forward in his defense of DuChesne. He should have kept his mind on his job. But at that moment he honestly didn't care why DuChesne had hired him, what he wanted, how much he was willing to pay Ray to bring Hollis to him. All that mattered was Hollis, what she'd endured, what she'd had to overcome to reach this point in her life.

"It was wrong, what DuChesne did to your mother," Ray said, surprised by the quiet indignation in his voice. "It was wrong for him to turn his back on her. Any man who'd turn his back on that kind of love is a fool."

Hollis appeared startled, as well. Her eyes flashed at him, large and round, green and silver. A laugh escaped her. "You work for him. You're supposed to be convincing me that deep down he's a good guy."

"Yeah, I work for him. But he was wrong. To abandon a woman like that—there's no excuse. It's just plain wrong. I don't blame you for hating him."

She shrugged and glanced away. "There are worse things in life than having a jerk for a father."

Ray had wondered why a woman as smart and talented and beautiful as Hollis Griffin had remained single and unattached into her late twenties. She had so much going for her, yet she lived alone in a tiny town on the edge of nowhere. Maybe, after the way DuChesne had treated her mother, Hollis simply didn't have any faith in men. Maybe she didn't like them.

Yet she'd certainly seemed to like Ray's kiss. He remembered the texture of her lips on his, the warmth of her breath, the lithe curves of her body as she leaned against him. The only thing that had stopped them from letting the kiss develop into something more was an unfortunately timely dose of common sense on her part.

She stared at a photograph that might have been a spherical explosion of white fireworks but was, Ray realized, an enlargement of a dandelion gone to seed. He stared at the photo, too. He saw the drop of moisture strike the table, just barely missing the print.

Glancing up, he caught her in the act of swabbing her cheek with her hand. He considered circling the table and taking her in his arms again, but he knew that if he did, he wouldn't be able to let her go.

Instead, he pulled a linen handkerchief from his pocket and handed it to her. She accepted it with a faint nod, and dabbed at her eyes. "This is all your fault," she grumbled.

"What's all my fault?"

"I haven't cried since my mother died. And now, all of a sudden, you barge into my life and I'm crying twice in one day."

"You wouldn't be crying if the tears weren't there to shed."

The few tears that escaped his handkerchief left glistening streaks on her skin. "I wouldn't be crying if

I didn't have you reminding me what a mess my life is."

"Your life is far from a mess, Hollis."

She gazed at him, her eyes bright and powerful despite their dampness, her long, dark lashes spiked with moisture. "Go ahead," she prompted him. "Finish the sentence."

He smiled in confusion. "I thought I had."

"My life is far from a mess," she quoted, "and I can make it even better by meeting my father."

"I wasn't going to say that."

"You were thinking it."

"No."

"We both know that's what you want from me."

Again he smiled, wryly this time. That she had the fortitude to challenge him even when she was weepy indicated just how strong she was, just how tough and stubborn. Just how desirable she was to a man like Ray, who liked tough, stubborn, strong women.

"What I want from you has nothing to do with your father," he murmured, unable to gaze into those amazing eyes of hers without feeling an ache in the pit of his abdomen, a tension in his thighs, a hollow longing in his soul. Dear God, what he wanted from her was as far from his job, DuChesne and the rest of it as anything he could imagine.

What he wanted was her mouth on his. Her body beneath his. Her hair splayed out on the pillow of his motel bed—or here, on this long smooth table in this brightly lit room. The hell with DuChesne, the hell with professional ethics, the hell with the dreadful luck he could bring down upon a woman if he let himself care too much.

He wanted Hollis.

Evidently she felt his longing. Possibly she shared it. She lowered her eyes and let out a long, wistful breath.

"I should go," he said.

"Ray..." She raised her eyes, and saw his desire mirrored in her face. She wanted him as much as he wanted her. In spite of what she'd gone through, in spite of what she'd told him about herself, in spite of who she was and who he was. She wanted him.

"You said it wasn't a good idea," he reminded her. "And I agreed."

"Then, yes. You'd better go."

She extended her hand across the table and returned his handkerchief. He stuffed it into his pocket, wishing he could ignore the wetness of her tears on it.

But long after he'd left her house, after he'd driven back through town to the motel, long after the handkerchief had dried out, he was still thinking about her tears. Her strength. Her beauty, and her determination, and her courage.

He was still thinking about how right it had felt to kiss her. How wrong it was to want her.

And how knowing it was wrong didn't seem to matter.

Chapter Six

It's only because he's a detective, she told herself.

She sat in the front room of Curry Copy, waiting for Jeff Curry to return with an inventory of his glossy stock. He'd assured her over the phone that he had an adequate supply to run off five hundred catalogs. But when she'd walked into his shop with her prints, he'd belatedly realized he ought to make sure his supplies were adequate to fill her order.

So she sat on a folding metal chair next to a pile of albums displaying sample wedding invitations, and thought about Ray Fargo when she should have been fretting over whether she'd be able to get the catalogs printed in time for her show.

What was it about Ray that had compelled her to talk about her childhood? Last night, she'd trusted him. Not because he'd fed her. Not, she acknowledged, because he'd kissed her—although the desire he'd unleashed inside her with one gentle kiss was another mystery for her to puzzle over.

Hollis didn't respond to men. Not that way. At least, she never had before she'd met Ray Fargo.

She wasn't a virgin; during her brief time in college, a persistent boyfriend had talked her into what, in all honesty, she'd wanted to be talked into. She had hoped to learn what could be so wonderful about the act that it had led her mother to toss aside her sense of self-preservation and become passionately involved with a heartless beast like DuChesne. Hollis had wanted to find out if sex was splendid enough to compensate for the selfishness of men and the damage they inflicted.

She'd slept with her boyfriend and decided no, it wasn't splendid enough.

She didn't know Ray well enough to judge his character. He didn't seem hell-bent on inflicting damage, and he'd acted reasonably unselfish so far. But he could afford to be nice while he was collecting a fee from Olivier DuChesne. Ray wasn't hanging around with Hollis out of the goodness of his heart.

He was a detective. It was his job to find out things. That was what last night—what every minute Ray had spent in Hollis's company during the past few days—was about: finding out things. Learning what made her tick. Figuring out a strategy for getting her to yield to Olivier DuChesne's will.

She hadn't let herself think along those lines last night. When Ray had made the decision to leave, she'd walked him up the stairs, thanked him again for bringing such a fine dinner and helping her with the prints, and listened to him protest that he hadn't done a damned thing except keep her company.

They had stood awkwardly at her front door, searching for a way to say goodbye. She'd mumbled something silly—"Drive safely," or some such inanity—but he'd remained silent, gazing down into her upturned face. She'd seen the emotion in his golden brown eyes; she'd sensed it. She'd felt his need, part widower's grief and part protectiveness toward Hollis, topped by a hefty dollop of healthy male lust.

It hadn't occurred to her then that he was a private investigator on a case. For one endless moment by her front door, with his mouth mere inches from hers and his eyes boring into her with astonishing power, Ray Fargo was just a man—a man unlike any other she'd ever met.

A man who could turn her on with a look, a smile, a touch, a kiss.

She couldn't understand how she'd managed to send him away, when all she'd wanted was for him to stay with her. As it was, she'd thought about him all night long, dreamed about him, reached into the dark, fancying that he was beside her—and sighing to discover herself alone. Every time she'd closed her eyes, she'd relived the feel of his lips on hers, moving with such tenderness, such sweet, painstaking care she wanted to moan from the unfamiliar blend of pleasure and frustration. She'd felt his hands closed around hers, his tall, strong body supporting hers, and her heart had pounded wildly. She'd punched the pillows and kicked the sheets and fought against the urge to telephone his motel, to implore him to come back to her house and prove that making love could be better than she'd ever dared to imagine.

She had no doubt that Ray Fargo was the man who could prove it.

"Boy, are you in luck!" Jeff called as he emerged from the storage room at the rear of the shop. "We've got plenty of glossy in stock."

Hollis shook her head clear. In two days she would be on her way to New York City for her first major gallery show. She couldn't afford to exhaust her supply of mental energy on Ray Fargo.

It was for that reason that she didn't bother to chastise Jeff for having told Ray where she'd gone camping. She wasn't positive Jeff was the culprit, but as an avid hiker, he'd been the one to tell Hollis about the beautiful pond. And he did have that moss print hanging on the wall of his shop.

But what was the point of complaining? One way or another, Ray would have gotten to her.

She crossed to the counter with her portfolio of prints. She and Jeff hunched over the neatly numbered stack. "Make sure they're in the right order," she instructed him. "I worked this out very precisely last night."

"Yeah, I see the numbers," Jeff assured her. "Great picture of you in the *Vanderville Vantage,* by the way."

"Thanks." She busied herself checking the order form to make sure he'd gotten the quantities correct.

"Our own Hollis Griffin—front-page news. Too bad the paper doesn't get wider circulation."

"I doubt the Vanderville newspaper can do much to get people to attend the show," she said. "Who besides me would bother to drive four hours just to see a bunch of photographs?"

"I wasn't thinking of the show," Jeff said, tearing off the top sheet of the order form and handing it to her. "I was thinking of all the guys who might see your picture and start drooling."

Hollis rolled her eyes. "One thing I could do without is men who drool. Are you sure you can get the catalogs done by tomorrow morning?"

"Tomorrow afternoon," Jeff corrected her. "I'm not a miracle worker, Hollis."

"Tomorrow afternoon. I appreciate your rushing it through."

"No problem."

She left the shop, unlocked her bicycle chain and swung one leg over the saddle. And saw Ray, emerging from Josie's Luncheonette diagonally across the street.

He saw her the instant she saw him. He wasn't smiling, but even in his unsmiling mode he was disturbingly attractive. The severe line of his mouth struck her not as grim but as sensual. The opaque darkness of his eyes intrigued her.

His lips twitched in a failed attempt at a grin. She wondered whether he was angry with her, and could think of no reason other than her reluctance to journey to New Orleans. Last night might have left him unfulfilled, but the decision for him to leave had been his as much as hers.

She waited, balanced on her bike, until he'd reached her side of the street. "Hi," he said.

"You look like someone on his way to a tax audit," she observed, prompting a faint smile.

"I'm someone in dire need of real coffee," he complained. "I've been trying to get used to the swill they serve there—" he gestured toward Josie's "—but dumping sugar into it only changes the taste from nothing to sweet nothing. I'm about ready to start sucking on coffee grounds."

Hollis made a face. Ray laughed. She did, too.

Their laughter waned at the same time. Perched on her bicycle seat, she found herself at eye level with his chest. In the balmy Indian-summer heat, he wore only a thick cotton T-shirt. She could visualize the contours of his chest beneath it, the sleek, hard surface, the solidity of his shoulders. She didn't have to imagine the curved muscles of his upper arms, the sinews of his forearms, his large hands and blunt-tipped fingers, the flat expanse of his stomach, his hips, his legs...

She clung to the handlebars until the temptation to touch him passed.

"I talked to your father today," he said.

She inferred from his somber tone that that, more than the quality of the coffee at Josie's, accounted for his somber mood. "Oh?" she said noncommittally.

"I'm worried about him. I think..." Ray meditated for a minute, stroking his thumb absently along his jawline.

Hollis wished she had the nerve to stroke her thumb there, too. Once again, she squeezed her hands tightly around the handlebars. "You think what?" she asked.

"He isn't well."

She peered up at Ray, doubt replacing trust in her mind. Was he toying with her emotions? Laying a guilt trip on her? "Don't do this, Fargo."

"I'm not doing anything," he said, his tone as subdued, as taut as hers. "I'm simply telling you. I have these conversations with him, and..." Again he paused, shaking his head, raking his hand through his hair and pushing the thick brown waves off his brow. "It's just... something odd."

"What?" She tried to remain skeptical, but Ray looked so troubled, it was hard for her not to feel uneasy, as well. "What do you mean, odd?"

"He wants to meet you," Ray began. He must have sensed that she was about to argue that her father had no right to want anything when it came to her, because he continued before she could speak. "I report to him every day, Hollis. And all he talks about is having you with him in New Orleans, having you spend time at Serault Manor. And yet, not once..." He drifted off, shaking his head once more, staring past Hollis at the traffic light on the corner.

"Not once what?" she asked, curious in spite of herself.

"Not once has he asked me what you look like," Ray said, then frowned. "I shouldn't be discussing this with you."

"Why not?"

"He's the one paying me. I work for him."

Yet despite his qualms, Ray was discussing it. She considered the possible reasons. Because he truly liked her and felt a kinship with her? Or because he felt it would make her more amenable to visiting her father? She didn't want to believe Ray could be so manipulative, but she had no reason *not* to believe it. If her father was as rich and powerful as Ray implied, he would have hired the best detective in New Orleans. Ray had to be exceptionally good at what he did, or Olivier DuChesne would have sent someone else after Hollis.

"So." She shrugged, pretending none of this interested her in the least. "Maybe he doesn't give a damn what I look like."

"Maybe." But Ray didn't sound convinced.

"Maybe he remembers what my mother looked like. I look a lot like her."

Ray continued to stare at the traffic light. "If he were healthy, I'd figure he was just self-absorbed, wrapped up in his own agenda. But the man is sick. I can't help but wonder whether he's thinking clearly. He sent me up here after you, he's paying me good money to stay here with you and yet he's never asked me to describe you."

"Why don't you send him the *Vanderville Vantage?*" she muttered. "Everyone in town seems to think that front-page picture of me was great."

"He doesn't want your photograph, Hollis. He wants you." The light switched from red to green, and Ray directed his gaze back to Hollis. "I shouldn't be telling you this."

"Why not? He's my father. I'm supposed to be what this whole thing is about."

"Maybe the next time I talk to him I ought to put y'all on the phone."

"Me?"

"Why not? You just said it yourself. He's your father."

"What would I say to him?"

A humorless grin curved his lips. "How about, 'Hi, Dad.'?"

She grimaced.

"I think... I think you're just an idea to him, not a flesh-and-blood person. Maybe if he heard your voice, you'd become more human to him."

"Maybe," she added wryly, "if he thought of me as a flesh-and-blood person, he'd understand why I'm not jumping at the chance to put my life on hold for him."

"Maybe," Ray agreed.

She sighed. She wasn't sure this was a good idea. What if she heard the man's voice and started screaming and swearing? What if she lashed out at him over all the hurt and misery he'd caused her mother?

It would serve him right if she did. "Okay," she said, swallowing the bitter taste that suddenly filled her mouth. Oh, she had plenty to tell her father, the man whose seed had created her but whose life had repudiated her very existence. "I'll talk with Olivier DuChesne."

IF HE HAD deliberately plotted to lure her to his motel room, he wouldn't have succeeded. If it had been an act designed solely to get her into bed, he would have suffered an attack of scruples—or she would have suffered a bout of common sense. It simply wouldn't have happened.

But bringing her here to telephone DuChesne was quite something else. It hadn't been premeditated, and it had nothing to do with his attraction to Hollis, which continued to pulse incessantly inside him. It had nothing to do with the fact that they were in the room—just the two of them and a big, wide bed—and he'd spent the better part of the previous night alone in that big, wide bed, wishing she was with him.

This was work. He was on the job, and when he was on the job his brain, not his hormones, ran the show.

He'd tossed her bike into his trunk and driven her to the motel. By the time they'd reached his room, her eyes were round and glassy, her lower lip bitten raw. He would have liked to believe that her nerves had resulted from being here with him. But he knew who owned her emotions right now: her father.

He crossed to the nightstand and pulled DuChesne's phone number from the file by the bed. Hollis paced the small room at a sprinter's clip, wringing her hands, obviously trying to shake off her jitters. Ray sent a silent prayer heavenward that, for all her worrying, her first conversation with her father proved to be an experience of transcendent joy.

Fat chance.

As he began to punch the digits on the phone, she took a seat beside him, causing the mattress to sink beneath his hips. Cripes, he thought, I'm on a bed with Hollis and I'm not making love to her. What's wrong with this picture?

Allowing himself a self-deprecating private laugh, he dialed the final digit. After several rings he heard the haughty, clipped voice of DuChesne's valet.

"This is Ray Fargo again," he said. "Is Mr. DuChesne available?"

"I shall see."

Ray was put on hold. He glanced at Hollis, who sat stiffly next to him, her hands white-knuckled in her lap and her teeth worrying her lower lip in a way that made Ray want to hang up the phone and move on to more entertaining diversions. But despite her obvious anxiety, she sat straight, her chin firmed, her eyes bright with determination.

She had to be the bravest woman he'd ever met. Her bravery, plus the way she kept gnawing on her lower lip, would have undone Ray if he'd been a weaker man. As it was, without an adequate dose of caffeine, he was hanging on to his self-control by a mere thread.

"Fargo." DuChesne's soft, raspy drawl reached him through the wire. "Y'all have news for me?"

"What I have," Ray said slowly, carefully, "is your daughter. She's sitting beside me right now. She'd like to talk to you."

DuChesne said nothing for a lengthy minute. Ray wasn't surprised; the poor man was probably in shock.

"She wants to talk to me?" DuChesne finally managed.

"That's right."

Another long silence. Ray wondered whether DuChesne had been traumatized to the point of death. He figured that if the man had keeled over, the British butler would let Ray know.

"Why don't you just say hello to her and see what transpires?" Ray urged him. "She's sitting right next to me."

"All right," DuChesne said, sounding even weaker. "Put her on. Let me talk to her."

Ray wouldn't have called DuChesne's tone particularly warm or paternal. But again, the man was clearly in a tenuous state, both physically and emotionally. No doubt he was saving what enthusiasm he had for his daughter.

Ray handed her the phone. Her eyes met his. They blazed with sheer panic. "It's all right," he mouthed, then put his arm around her shoulders because she seemed in grave need of comforting.

He noticed the slight tremor in her hand as she lifted the phone to her ear. "Hello?" she half spoke, half whispered.

He couldn't hear DuChesne's voice through the receiver. He couldn't begin to conjecture what DuChesne was saying. All he knew was that Hollis's shoulders were as stiff as cold metal within the curve of his arm, that her face was chalky, that her lower lip was quivering again. And that her eyes continued to blaze.

"That's right," Hollis said. "She passed away seven years ago."

She listened. Her shoulders seemed to grow impossibly stiffer. She hunched forward, and Ray assumed she no longer wanted his arm around her.

He rose and stalked to the window. Gazing out at the stretch of asphalt, he couldn't see her. But he could envision her, clinging to the phone, curling her hands around it, contorting her body into a self-protective knot. He could hear her breathless voice saying, "I'm really very busy right now. I just don't see how I could come down there," and, "I understand. Mr. Fargo has told me," and, "I don't know. I'm sorry, I don't— This is very hard for me." And finally, "Please, don't say anything more. Okay? Just don't say anything more."

Another silence, then he heard her murmur a faint goodbye. Then a quiet click as she hung up the phone.

He turned slowly, pulling a fresh handkerchief from his pocket to mop up the tears he fully expected her to be shedding.

She wasn't crying. She was seated where he'd left her, her elbows on her knees and her head propped in her hands, her gaze focused on the cheap carpet at her feet.

"Are you all right?" he asked.

She lifted her eyes. They were turbulent with confusion, with doubt. Not a hint of dampness, of love or regret or penitence. "Who was that?" she asked, gesturing toward the phone.

The question took him aback. "Your father."

"How do I know that?"

What the hell was she getting at? "Why wouldn't it be your father?" he asked, suddenly as wary as she was.

She stood and stared at him. "I don't know. For all I know, you could have set up that call with an accomplice. You could have hired an actor, someone who can sound sickly and do a good Louisiana accent. For all I know, this could be a big hoax. You'd try anything to get me to go to New Orleans, wouldn't you?"

Damn. She was smart, maybe smarter than he was, to have imagined such a scheme. "That was your father," he insisted, taking a cautious step toward her.

He could see her warring with herself, trying to refrain from more pacing and hand-wringing. "I don't believe you," she said, her voice taut, strained from the effort to hold her emotions in. "I don't believe you, Ray Fargo. And now I'm going to leave. Unlock the trunk of your car, please. I'd like to get my bicycle."

"It's too long a distance for you to bike home," he argued, wishing he could think of a better reason to keep her from leaving.

"I'd like to get my bicycle," she repeated, standing before the door and staring at him, exuding fury and fear and the most astonishing dignity he'd ever witnessed.

"All right." He capitulated. To deny her request would be like denying an eagle its freedom. More than ever, he wanted her to stay. But he wouldn't keep her from leaving.

He opened the door, walked with her to the rental car and unlocked the trunk. Without looking at him, she pulled the bike out, straddled it, set her purse in the little straw basket and pedaled away.

And for the first time since his wife had died, Ray felt as if he'd lost the only thing of value in his life.

Chapter Seven

Of course. The whole thing was a fraud. A setup. Ray Fargo wasn't a private investigator, and that man—that drawling, tissue-thin voice on the telephone line—wasn't her father. For whatever reason, someone wanted to harass her, wanted to turn her into a nervous wreck, wanted to get her to New Orleans for some nefarious purpose. Someone had planned this elaborate hoax.

She wondered who—and why.

She wished she could shake from her mind the death-echoing rasp of that man's voice, and her last shred of credence that Ray Fargo was truly who he said he was. If only she could prove that her father wasn't dying, didn't want to see her, didn't give a damn about her, she could get on with her life.

She *could* prove it. In fact, she was ashamed of herself for having not thought of confirming Ray's story sooner.

The four-mile bike ride from his motel to her house tired her out, but her compulsion to erase this entire sorry episode from her life energized her. She stormed into the kitchen, where she'd left the business card Ray had given her the first time they'd met.

She went into her bedroom and dialed the long-distance number printed at the bottom. After two rings, a woman answered. "Fargo Private Investigations. May I help you?" Her accent resembled Ray's—and that of the man who claimed to be Olivier DuChesne.

"May I speak to Mr. Fargo, please?" Hollis asked.

"I'm afraid he's out of the office. If y'all would like to leave your name and number—"

"I'd rather try him again later. What time will he be back?"

"I can't rightly say," the woman replied. "He's on a case out of town. If you need immediate assistance, I could pass your number along to him and have him get back to you. Or I could recommend another investigator."

"No, that's okay. Thanks anyway." Hollis lowered the phone, then dropped onto her bed and meditated.

Perhaps the woman was just another accomplice. Perhaps she was sitting right next to the frail-sounding man who'd posed as Olivier DuChesne, and using the very same telephone.

Hollis needed more proof. She dialed Directory Assistance and requested the telephone number of police headquarters in Lafayette, Louisiana.

Within minutes, she was connected to someone in the personnel department there. "Hello," she said, joining the ranks of Ray's telephone-imposter cohorts. "I'm calling about a man named Ray Fargo. I understand he was a police detective in Lafayette until a few years ago."

"What precinct?" asked the bored-sounding man on the other end of the line.

"I don't know." Hollis thought fast. "He's under consideration for employment with my firm, and his résumé says he worked for a while on the Lafayette police force. He ended his career there as a detective. Can you confirm this?"

"What was the name again?"

"Fargo. Ray Fargo."

"Hold on a sec."

She was placed on hold for a good deal longer than a second. Just when impatience was about to get the better of her, the man returned to the line. "Yes, ma'am. He did serve on the force here, until six years ago."

"I see." She strove to sound official. "Can you relate the reasons for his dismissal?"

"He wasn't dismissed, ma'am. He quit."

"Can you tell me why?"

The man weighed his answer. "Personal reasons," he finally said.

"As a potential employer—" she pressed him "—I'd really like to know."

"I can't release that information. It's personal."

Hollis scrambled for a new tactic. "He mentioned to me that he might have had a problem with alcohol."

The personnel manager chuckled. "That wasn't why he left, ma'am. He was a good cop—excellent record, several citations for valor. Never drank on the job."

"That's reassuring," she said. "But I'm concerned—"

"Our records contain nothing about him having any problem with liquor. He left the force for personal reasons." Evidently the man felt a surge of generosity, because he added, "There was a family tragedy, ma'am."

His wife's death.

She sighed. Ray's story appeared to check out.

She thanked the man and hung up the phone. A shudder passed through her as she acknowledged that if Ray's story was true, then the rest was probably true, too. The person she'd spoken to on the phone in Ray's motel room was her father.

And he was dying. She'd heard it in his quavering voice, in the wheeze and whistle of his breath, in the unspoken plea underlining his words. The last of her family was dying—unless she counted DuChesne's twin children, the half brother and half sister she would meet only if she was willing to travel to New Orleans.

A sob rose to her throat, but she resolutely swallowed it. She would not weep for that man who had never once wept for her and her mother. She would not feel an obligation to him, just because he wanted to see her before he passed away. She would not be an obedient daughter to the father she had never known.

She would continue to live her life as she always had: looking forward, taking charge, not letting the mistakes of others limit her choices or determine her course. She had herself, and that had always been enough in the past. It would be enough now.

But Olivier DuChesne was dying. She'd heard the echo of his mortality, and her own. He was her blood. Her heritage.

Her father.

The sob rose into her throat; she tasted the salt of unshed tears. Her hands felt icy; she rubbed them together and took a deep breath.

Why cry for her father? Had he ever cried for her?

She had no good reason to trust Olivier DuChesne—but she'd lost her reason not to trust Ray. He had been telling her the truth all along, a truth she didn't want to hear but one he had refused to let her deny.

"The show," she said aloud, pushing away from the bed. Whatever happened between her and her father wasn't going to happen until after her show. She wasn't going to think about it. She wasn't going to let that bastard ruin the most important event of her professional life.

She would worry about him later, him and Ray Fargo both. Right now, all that mattered was keeping her life on track and her mind as sharply focused as her telephoto lens.

All that mattered was remembering who she was and how she'd gotten here, who'd been with her for the journey and who hadn't.

All that mattered was knowing whom to trust.

"YOU LOOK LIKE HELL," Sheila said, glancing away from the road long enough to give Hollis a quick appraisal.

Even without the overcast afternoon sky to lend her face a ghostly pallor, Hollis knew she looked dreadful. She'd winced at her reflection in the mirror that morning. Her eyes were framed in such deep shadows that she resembled a raccoon; her lips were chapped, and smiling required a superhuman effort.

She wasn't feeling particularly superhuman.

She had asked Sheila to drive her to the print shop. She would have taken her van, but she hadn't finished loading her prints for her trip to New York. She should have had them all packed by now, but she was way behind schedule. Just one more thing to augment an already ghastly mood.

She supposed her state of mind wasn't surprising. In the best of circumstances she would be a bundle of nerves—happy nerves, maybe, but one didn't approach one's debut into the New York City art world without some anxiety. And these weren't the best of circumstances.

She hadn't slept more than ten minutes total last night. She hadn't eaten. She hadn't listened to her own admonition to forget about her father and Ray.

Especially Ray.

Even when she refused to let her father enter her mind, she couldn't stop thinking about Ray, about how she'd been wrong to distrust him, about how his wife's death had caused him to leave the police force. About how, when his arms closed around her and his lips caressed hers, she felt longings she had never felt before, sensations she had never known existed.

She was glad Sheila was driving. Even with four cups of coffee polluting her bloodstream, she wouldn't trust her reflexes behind the wheel.

"I guess I'm stressed out about tomorrow," she told her friend.

"Are you sure?" Sheila shoved her thick blond hair back from her face, giving Hollis an unobstructed view of her scowl. "You may be stressed out, but are you sure it all has to do with tomorrow? I talked to my cousin Chet a couple of days ago."

Hollis rolled her eyes. "I haven't seen him in months."

"He told me that. He really likes you, you know," Sheila remarked. "He did happen to mention that you're a cold fish."

Not with Ray Fargo, I'm not, Hollis almost blurted out. "If that's what Chet said, who am I to argue?" she said in a deceptively bland voice. "Sorry, Sheila, I know you'd love it if he and I got together, but it just isn't meant to be."

"What's the matter with you, Hollis? Chet is the best catch in Washington County. If he weren't my cousin, I'd go after him myself."

"I read an article recently that said scientists have decided there aren't any serious genetic risks when cousins marry."

"Hollis. We're talking about you, not me."

Hollis cursed under her breath. She didn't want to talk about herself. She'd been trying very hard not even to think about herself. "Here's the deal, Sheila," she said. "Chet is a good-looking man. But there's just no...no chemistry. No magic."

"You want magic?"

"I'm not going to settle for anything less," Hollis said, wishing with all her heart that Ray's face didn't materialize in her mind, his body didn't fill her imagination, her body didn't clench in response. Why on earth did she believe Ray could offer her that magic? She loathed the man.

Sighing wearily, she stared out the window. She had never before been so happy to see the bright yellow Curry Copy Center sign loom into view.

"I know Chet can be a bore," Sheila conceded. "But anyway, he isn't the problem. It's *you* I'm really worried about."

"Do me a favor—don't worry about me."

"You ought to work some things out in your head, Hollis. Like why you need to keep every man who's interested in you at arm's length."

There was only one man Hollis felt that need with—and that was because he was the only man she could ever imagine getting too close to her. "Why is everyone so keen on psychoanalyzing me?" she muttered. "You're a good friend, Sheila, but you're really getting on my nerves. Can we bring this discussion to a close?"

"For the time being." Sheila steered the car into a parking space and turned off the engine. "Do you want me to come in with you?"

"You don't have to. If the box is too heavy I'll have Jeff carry it out for me."

"Okay." Sheila got out of the car, but only to light a cigarette. She sat on the hood of the car, propped her feet on the bumper, and sent Hollis a sheepish grin before Hollis could lecture her on the evils of smoking.

Shaking her head, Hollis strode to the front door of the print shop. The bell above the door announced her entrance.

Jeff Curry glanced up from the offset printer and smiled at her. "The catalogs came out great!" he announced. "Wait till you see them. They're beautiful."

For the first time since she'd spoken to her father—for the first time, in fact, since Ray Fargo had invaded Vanderville—she felt as if her life were back in sync. If her catalogs were beautiful, everything would fall into place. Her show would be a success, Ray would give up on her and go back to New Orleans and she would receive word that her father had experienced a miraculous recovery and she should feel free to visit him at her convenience. Everything, like the catalogs, would come out great.

She waited eagerly as Jeff turned off his printer and vanished into the back room. He returned to the counter with a bulky carton cradled in his arms. Setting it down with a thump, he pulled back the flaps and handed her a catalog.

Gingerly, almost reverently, she thumbed through the photographs. Objectively, she noted how clearly they'd reproduced, how crisp the images appeared on the slick paper. Subjectively, she wanted to dance with pleasure. Here was her proof that her luck was changing, that her life was back within her control and she was moving in the right direction. Nothing—not her ailing, neglectful father, not her childhood struggles and losses, not Ray Fargo—could alter the fact that Hollis was a great photographer on the cusp of professional triumph.

She could barely calm down enough to write a check for the cost of the printing. Leaving out one catalog so she could show it to Sheila, Jeff taped down the flaps of the box. He handed Hollis her receipt, and she slid the carton over the counter and into her arms.

"It's heavy," Jeff warned, starting around the counter. "You want me to lug it outside for you?"

"No." It *was* heavy, but Hollis felt a proprietary thrill in carrying it herself. "If you can just get the door for me—"

"I've got it" came a familiar husky voice.

Spinning around, Hollis found herself gazing into Ray Fargo's eyes. In her shock, she fumbled the carton.

He smoothly lifted it out of her arms. "Here's a better idea," he said, his drawl as thick as molasses. "You get the door for me. I'll bring it outside."

She would have challenged him, swiped the carton out of his hands and maybe kicked him in the shins for good measure. But she didn't want to make a scene in front of Jeff. Squaring her shoulders and sending Ray what she hoped was a lethal frown, she yanked the door open. The tinkle of the bell mocked her anger.

As it was, she wasn't quite sure why she was angry with Ray—except that when he was near she couldn't think of anything but him. The beautiful catalogs, her show, her pride in her accomplishments—everything was eclipsed by him, a great, blinding darkness moving across her bright horizon. He reminded her of everything she wanted to ignore, everything she wanted to forget: her father, her loneliness, her inability to respond to a handsome man like Sheila's cousin Chet—or, for that matter, to any man but Ray.

"Where am I taking this?" he asked pleasantly as the door swung shut behind them.

She pointed toward Sheila's car. Surprised, Sheila sprang down from the fender and crushed her cigarette under the heel of her sneaker. "You want me to open the trunk?" she asked, her eyes never leaving Ray.

"Yes, please," Hollis said tersely. Damn it, but she'd been so thrilled just a moment ago, when she'd seen her photographs printed in the catalog. She hadn't been ready to lose that brief elation. She didn't want to think about Ray.

She had no choice. He was here, and she could think of nothing but him.

She trailed him around to the rear of the car, where Sheila stood fidgeting with her keys. The latch gave way, and Ray lowered the carton into the trunk. Ignoring Sheila, he lifted the catalog from Hollis's numb fingers. "Mind if I have a look?"

"Yes," she said, although he was already thumbing through it. "I do mind."

"I helped y'all with it," he reminded her. "I want to see how it came out."

"He helped you?" Sheila asked, obviously eager to learn more about the mystery man in Hollis's life.

"Sheila—" Hollis reluctantly introduced them "—this is Ray Fargo. Ray, my friend Sheila Robbins." Before they'd finished shaking hands, Hollis launched into an attack. "I've got a million things to do, Ray. I haven't got time to stand around here—"

"Then go," he said amiably. "I can drop this off at your house when I'm done looking at it."

"I don't want you at my house." Her fury seemed to erupt from some unknown place inside her and overflow like hot lava, scorching everything in its path. "Please, Ray—I'm hanging on by a thread. Just stay away from me."

He gazed at her, his affable smile replaced by a look of grave concern. "You aren't going to snap, darlin', are you?"

She was appalled to admit to herself how close she was to snapping. "How much is he paying you?"

Again Ray's expression changed, this time from concerned to guarded. He knew to whom she was referring. "My usual rate," he said laconically.

"And what might that be?"

"What does it matter, Hollis? That's between him and me."

"I want to know. I want to know how much that man is paying you to lurk around Curry Copy Center until I show up. I want to know how much I'm worth to him."

"A lot."

"How much?"

A pregnant minute stretched between them. Hollis was scarcely aware that Sheila was standing no more than a couple of feet away. All she was aware of was Ray, his honey-brown eyes and his athletic physique and the tension that sizzled in the air between him and herself.

She was feeling more than just anger, she acknowledged. More than just fear, more than just the dread of seeing her carefully wrought life crumble into dust.

She was feeling desire—a wild, illogical, utterly unfamiliar desire for Ray Fargo. Desire sparked by that one kiss in her kitchen. Desire fed by the hours she'd spent with him, telling him things she never told anyone. Desire nourished by the tears she'd wept in his presence, in his arms.

She hated him. He had done nothing to earn her hatred—except to appear one morning in front of the Vanderville post office and demolish her universe. But she hated him anyway, for making her lose her grip, for making her think things she'd never wanted to think and feel things she'd never wanted to feel.

"Five hundred dollars a day, plus expenses," he said.

She stared at him. She managed to remain perfectly still while her soul reeled at the understanding that this was the value her father attached to her. It seemed like an awful lot of money—and much, much too little.

The quaking in her heart expanded until shivers racked her body. Praying that Ray couldn't see how completely shaken she was, she pivoted on her heel, marched around the car to the passenger side and climbed in, giving the door a hinge-rattling slam. In the side mirror she observed as Sheila and Ray exchanged a few words, as he tucked the catalog possessively under his arm, as Sheila shrugged and grinned and gave him a wave. Then he headed down the street and Sheila strolled around to the driver's side.

She settled in behind the wheel, and the car filled with the aromas of sour September air and stale cigarette smoke. "Okay, Hollis," she said cheerfully. "Tell me what the hell that was all about."

Hollis stewed. Again she chided herself for having directed her fury at Ray. He was only the agent of change, not the cause of it. He was only doing Olivier DuChesne's bidding.

For five hundred dollars a day, plus expenses.

"There's nothing to tell," she mumbled.

Sheila gave her an incredulous look.

"I'm sorry."

"You're in love with him."

Hollis lurched. Only her seat belt kept her in place. "I hate his guts."

Sheila grinned and eased out of the parking space. "I'll tell Chet to give up."

"I can think of nothing that would make me happier," Hollis muttered, refusing to acknowledge her friend's dismissal of her claim that she hated Ray.

She said nothing more during the ten-minute drive to her house. What could she say, other than that Ray Fargo had caused her more upheaval than she could stand, that he was in a position to bring her more pain—or more joy—than she'd ever experienced in her life, that his very existence was forcing her to redefine who she was, where she was going and what her life meant.

And he was doing it all for five hundred dollars a day, plus expenses.

FROM WHERE SHE KNELT inside her van, the sound of his engine was muffled, almost indiscernible as he coasted to a halt in her driveway. But somehow she had known he would show up. She'd been expecting him.

Not that she'd done anything to prepare herself for his visit. She had on the blue jeans and oversize T-shirt she'd been wearing all day. Smudges of dust marred her knees, and her hair was mussed, tucked behind her ears. Once she had everything loaded into the van, she intended to take a long shower, wash her hair and pack a small bag for tomorrow. Suzanne, the gallery owner, had promised her access to a private lounge at the gallery so she could pretty herself up for the party.

Knowing intuitively that Ray was going to show up at her house sometime before the day ended, she could have prettied herself up for him. But sheer stubbornness prevented her. She was still too busy hating him—and reassuring herself that it was all right to hate him for turning her world upside down, even though he was only doing his job.

She remained by the open rear doors of her van, glowering at him as he coasted up the driveway, yanked on the parking brake and shut off the engine. She wished she could intimidate him with her frown. If only he weren't quite so tall, so intent. If only his legs didn't carry him with such efficient grace to the edge of the carport.

"I brought y'all your catalog," he said, extending the book to her.

The dusk light threw his face into shadow. Her vision traced his outline, the broad shoulders, the loose blazer, the snug denim jeans. "You could have kept it."

"You'll need it in New York tomorrow."

"If I'm lucky," she muttered. "If enough people bother to show up."

"Oh, Hollis, they're going to be lined up down the street to get in. I've been studying this thing all afternoon, just going through it page by page. These photos are wonderful."

"Delta silt," she said flatly, leaping down from the rear of the van and edging past him.

She couldn't quite see his face in the dim twilight, but she could feel the impact of his smile. She could imagine the dent of his dimple, the shimmering warmth of his eyes, the scent of his soap mingled with the pungent fragrance of pine in the cool air.

"I didn't bring dinner tonight," he said.

"It's just as well. I'm not hungry."

"You really ought to stop and catch your breath. You don't want to be frazzled tomorrow."

"I'll be fine." *Especially if you leave right now, so I can put you out of my mind.*

He was still holding the catalog, his arm slightly extended. "I wish you didn't despise me," he murmured.

His voice was too husky, too sexy. The only way she could combat its effect on her was to despise him. "I wish you didn't let my father pay you to destroy my life."

"I'm not trying to destroy anything."

She stared at the catalog in his outstretched hand, wondering if there was a way to take it from him without her fingers brushing his.

Before she could muster the courage to take the damned thing, he tossed it into her van and closed the doors. "I thought having you talk to him would help," he said.

"Well, it didn't." She heard the catch in her voice and cleared her throat. "What you thought was that having me talk to him would make me feel sorry for him."

Ray lounged against the van, his arms folded and one ankle crossed over the other, as casual as if it were his van, in his carport. The sunset's pink residue washed his face. She could see him clearly now, too clearly—the ironic twist of his smile, the mesmerizing undertow of his gaze. "Pretty clever of me, wasn't it?"

It pained her to admit how effective his ploy had been. That pain erupted in fresh anger. "Why won't you leave me alone?"

"You know why."

Five hundred dollars a day plus expenses, that was why. "The first day I met you, I considered having you arrested for stalking me. Maybe now's the time to do it."

"I'm not stalking you. I'm just bringing you that catalog."

"Thanks. You brought it. Now go away."

"Is this what's known as Northern hospitality?"

Damn his smile. Damn the dazzling light in his eyes, the virile power of his stance, his uncanny knack for goading her. "I mean it, Ray—"

"Y'all don't mean it," he argued, his tone hushed and gentle, his drawl in overdrive. "Y'all really want to mend fences with your daddy before he dies. Don't you, Annabelle?"

The thread she'd been hanging by snapped at the sound of his voice wrapped around that despised name. Her sanity snapped. Her tension. Her control.

Before she realized what she was doing, she swung her hand, slapping him across the cheek.

The sound of the smack startled her even more than the warm, slightly bristly texture of his skin against her palm. The sudden stillness shocked her. Her own violence horrified her. The iron-hard lock of his hand around her wrist should have frightened her, but it didn't. She knew he would not hit her back.

His gaze was hard, tight on her face as he yanked on her arm, pulling her closer. He stared into her eyes, all traces of humor gone from his face. His breath was as harsh as hers, his rage palpable. "Annabelle," he said, his voice dark, ominous.

"Don't call me that."

"It's your name. Annabelle."

She reached back to swing with her free hand. He easily manacled her other wrist with his strong, strong fingers.

"Annabelle," he whispered.

She would not cry. Never again, not for him. "That's his mother's name," she said, her voice taut, gritty with hostility. "My mother named me in honor of Olivier DuChesne's mother because she thought maybe then he'd accept me. She would have done anything to make him accept me—even name me after that sonofabitch's mother. I hate the name Annabelle. If you ever call me that again—"

His lips crushed down on hers, fierce and silencing. He hauled her against him, trapped her fists between their bodies, wedged her hips between his thighs, and she felt a strange fire leap through her, fury and despair and need warring for dominance inside her.

His mouth was hot and hungry, his tongue pushing past the barrier of her lips. A token protest gathered in her throat, then dissolved into a moan as her tongue met the searing thrusts of his, as she unfurled her hands and pressed them to his chest, probing the muscled surface through the cotton of his shirt.

A faint groan escaped him, and she understood in that instant, before she gave herself fully to his kiss, that his anger had vanished. So, she acknowledged, had hers. All that was left was the need, sweet and passionate—his need as much as hers.

She had never much enjoyed kissing—and *enjoy* didn't seem the right word for how she felt about this kiss. It overwhelmed her, it shattered her, it made her feel weak and strong at the same time. She wanted Ray to take all of her the way he had taken her mouth. She wanted him inside her, inhabiting her. She wanted to make him as weak, as strong, as she felt at that moment.

As her fingers roamed across his chest, he released her wrists and skimmed his hands down her sides, around her waist. When he'd kissed her in her kitchen he'd been gentle, comforting, arousing her with tenderness. This kiss was demanding, impolite, not questioning but conquering.

He moved his hands lower, to her bottom, and drew her against him. Through his jeans and hers she felt his arousal and her own helplessness, her inability to resist, her failure to hate this man.

She surged closer. Her body ached to feel his hardness against her. At her uncertain motion he moaned something—an oath, a promise, a plea. Tugging her shirt free of her slacks, he slipped his hands underneath. His callused fingertips sketched tingly lines across the warm skin of her back, making her shiver and rock her hips to his.

"I want you," he whispered, his hips surging in time with hers. He drew his hands forward, rising to her bra and massaging her breasts through the thin fabric.

A tortured cry escaped her as her nipples stiffened. For a moment she was frightened—not of Ray but of this, the unknown, the sensation that she was perched precariously on the verge of something, that she wanted nothing more than to tumble over and down into it, with Ray. Only Ray.

His mouth opened against hers again, as eager as before. His tongue swept her mouth, glided over her teeth and tangled with her tongue. She felt the muscles in his thighs flex and tense against her. "I want to love you," he said, softer than a sigh.

Love. Just hearing him say the word, even if he didn't mean it, even if what they were feeling at that moment, what they were sharing, had nothing to do with commitment and forever...

"I want you to love me, Ray...."

Her voice faltered and she sensed a change in him. His hands glided slowly down to the edge of her shirt and out. His head fell back until he was staring at the rafters of the carport's roof. His chest pumped erratically; his legs still sandwiched her hips. But gradually, achingly, he withdrew.

"I can't do this," he said.

A sudden spasm of conscience? A decision that he couldn't make love to her while he was taking money from her father?

Or did he just not want her, after all?

"You're trying to make me lose my mind," she guessed, dismayed by the quiver in her voice.

He shook his head. His smile was heartbreakingly sad. "It's my mind that's lost, Hollis. I can't...I can't do this."

"Why?" Her boldness astonished her, yet she couldn't bear the idea that, just as she'd been about to break through, to discover love in the way a man like

Ray meant it, he was deliberately depriving her of the chance. "Why can't you do this?"

He lifted his hand to her cheek and brushed back an errant strand of hair. Even that fleeting contact seemed to trouble him. He straightened up, nudged her away and moved to safety a few steps from her. "I'll doom you," he said, his tone as bleak as his gaze.

"That sounds a bit melodramatic."

"I don't care what it sounds like. It's the truth."

He seemed deadly serious. She couldn't fathom what he meant. "Because of my father?" she asked, groping for an explanation.

He shook his head. His expression was desolate, his mouth a grim line, his eyes as cold now as they were warm before. "Because of me. I'm no good, Hollis. I can't let myself care."

Her confusion increased. If she were more worldly, more experienced, perhaps she would know what he was talking about. "What can't you let yourself care about?"

"The last time I cared about a woman..." He gazed past Hollis and into the shadows, seeing something invisible to her. "She wound up dead."

"Your wife?"

"Yes."

"That was years ago."

"Yes."

At long last the molten heat he'd unleashed inside her cooled enough that she could follow his train of thought. Her passion waned, leaving in its wake a mournful emptiness, something bigger and deeper and more painful than any loneliness she'd ever known before.

She forced herself to forget her own frustration. "You haven't been with a woman since your wife died?"

"I'm not a saint, Hollis," he said quietly. "I've been with women. But I didn't care about them, not the same way."

She inferred a compliment in his statement, a hint that he cared about her more than he'd cared about the other women he'd known since his wife died. She'd thought she had gone insane, wanting Ray as much as she did, becoming obsessed with him, losing sleep over him, spending her rage and her tears on him. But perhaps he had gone just as insane over her.

"I'm not going to die, Ray."

Engaged in an inner struggle, he shook his head. "If we get too close, you might. It's my fault my wife died, Hollis. My fault. If it weren't for loving me, she'd be alive today."

A ripple of ice traveled the length of Hollis's spine. "What are you saying, Ray? Did you kill her?"

The sorrow in his eyes cut through her flesh to impale her soul. "I've asked myself that question too many times to count. And the only answer I've got is yes. I killed her."

Chapter Eight

The rational move might have been to sneak inside the house and call the police. But Ray *was* the police, or at least he had been once. And anyway, Hollis trusted him.

How could she not trust him? If he had wanted to hurt her, he would never have told her anything about his wife.

They sat side by side on the steps leading to the front door. The porch light needed a new bulb, but even if it were working, she wouldn't have turned it on. The evening's gloom and the long, taupe shadows spreading over the yard seemed more appropriate. A low breeze sifted through the trees, tugging orange pine needles from their branches and scattering them across the ground.

"You didn't really kill her, did you?" she asked.

Beside her, Ray sat motionless, his arms propped on his knees and his gaze fixed on a birch tree, a shocking streak of white among the gray trunks of the pines. His face gave nothing away, but she could feel his tension. She could sense it in his stillness, in the quiet flexing of his fingers, the jut of his jaw.

"She died because of me."

"That's not the same thing."

"Isn't it?"

Again his fingers flexed. Hollis watched, mesmerized by their strength, their motion, the ridge of his knuckles, the protrusions of his wrist bones.

"She took a bullet for me," he said, his voice hushed, whispering with sorrow and remorse.

"What do you mean?"

"*I* was supposed to die, Hollis. Not her. The bullet was meant for me."

Hollis inhaled deeply, fighting off the icy shivers that racked her. She hadn't lived a sheltered life, but in her mind, death had always been associated with car crashes, or maybe illness. Not bullets.

"This was when you were a policeman."

He nodded. His eyes remained on the birch tree near the road. "I was a good cop. Denise was a good cop's wife. She was a social worker. She worked with juveniles, so she understood what I was dealing with. She never fretted for me, never reproached me or asked me to quit the force the way other wives did."

He had loved his wife, Hollis comprehended. He didn't have to say it; she could hear the love in his voice as clearly as if he'd spoken the actual words. She wondered if he still loved his wife today, years after her death.

She wondered why the possibility caused her a twinge of envy.

"I was a detective in vice, and I'd broken up a drug ring and run several people in. One of them who wasn't picked up during the bust came gunning for me." He lapsed into silence, as if reliving the incident in his head. Hollis could see his shoulders tightening. She could hear his breath growing rough. "He shot her at our house. That place should have been sacred. But nothing is sacred to them. They don't care. They want you dead, and they come after you. They see something and they shoot, and they just don't give a damn who's in the way or who they've hit or what terrible pain they bring...."

Again his voice faltered.

"You don't have to tell me."

He continued, anyway. "I had a hat, an old duck-bill cap with the name of my father's favorite hardware store printed above the rim. Denise was always teasing me about it because I wore it so damned much. She was clowning around one evening, and she put on the cap, mimicking me, and struck a pose by the window. I reckon she made a silhouette against the drape. And that man, that murderer..."

"Ray." She wished he would stop. She couldn't bear to hear the rest. She couldn't bear to hear the raw agony in his words, his voice.

He refused to spare her. "He saw the cap, and he took aim and fired."

Another shiver tore through Hollis. If his wife had been clowning around, he must have been in the room, watching her performance. And if he'd been there, he'd watched her get shot. He'd seen the bullet enter the window, enter the body of the woman he loved.

"I'm so sorry, Ray," she murmured, horribly aware of the insufficiency of her words. She wanted to take his hand, kiss his cheek, offer him whatever reassurance he would accept.

Just minutes ago she'd been ready to invite him into her bed. But now she felt a wall between them, invisible but real. Her only option was to try to break through that wall and reach him somehow.

"It must have been awful for you," she said.

He let out a humorless laugh. "It must have been. I honestly don't remember."

"Did you block it out?"

"Lord knows I tried. I tried drinking. I tried traveling. I went home to Terrebonne Parish and scraped and sanded my father's boat till I'd all but rubbed the skin off my hands. When I was finally done running away, a year had come and gone and I was in New Orleans. I figured there was no sense going back to Lafayette. I had nothing left there."

"Ray." Her arms ached to hold him, to cradle and comfort him with the promise that everything would be all right. But the wall remained between them, towering and unbreachable, locking him within its boundaries. And everything *wouldn't* be all right. His wife was dead; that would never change. "It isn't your fault."

"What isn't my fault? Denise's death? Of course it's my fault."

"You didn't kill her."

"If she hadn't been my wife she'd be alive today."

"Yes. And if my mother hadn't been on the road at the same time as an eighteen-wheeler with lousy brakes, she'd be alive today, too."

"It's not the same thing." He sounded impatient, his tone devoid of the sultry warmth she adored. "She took my bullet. Do you understand what that means?"

Evidently Hollis didn't. "It means she saved your life," she guessed.

"It means I brought that death down on her. It means..." At last he looked at Hollis squarely, his eyes dark and fierce. "It means that she died because she chose the wrong man to love."

"But you didn't do anything—"

"I did *everything,*" he retorted, his voice slicing through the tranquil evening. "I brought danger and death into her life. I don't know why it happened the way it did, but it was *my* danger, and it cost her her life." He turned away, and when he next spoke he sounded weary. "I'm not going to let some other good woman die because of me, Hollis. You'd be safer keeping your distance from me."

She stared at the birch tree, her gaze paralleling his. The night's gathering darkness pressed down on her, heavy and mournful. She didn't want to keep her distance from Ray. She wanted to be close to him, as close as he would let her come.

If she were able to view the situation objectively, she would realize he was right to push her away. Not because he posed any real threat to her—at least not the sort of threat that would result in her death—but because his life was in Louisiana and hers was in upstate New York, because he was her father's agent and she detested her father.

Because if she *did* get close to him, he would only wind up leaving her, and she would wind up with a broken heart.

All right. He had his reasons, she had hers, but they both had to embrace the same conclusion. "I guess you'd better go, then," she said, her voice as devoid of light as the shadows devouring the yard.

"Yes. I'd better." He stood, adjusted his jacket with a shrug and then took her hands in his and lifted her to her feet. Despite everything he'd told her—or maybe because of it—the power of his hands folded around hers unleashed a tide of pain and longing and regret through her.

She didn't want him to go.

He must have read the misery in her eyes. "Don't be angry with me, Hollis. I'm saving you from the worst fate there is."

Loving Ray Fargo couldn't be that terrible a fate. Or maybe it could.

It didn't matter. He had chosen to save her from it.

"I hope tomorrow goes well for you," he added, releasing her hands and taking a step backward.

Tomorrow. Her show in New York.

How strange that the most important step in her career had faded to insignificance in her mind. Who cared about the show? Ray had just let her glimpse his soul. And before he'd done that, he had let her glimpse her own soul, that secret, passionate core of her that had needed only the right man to come along and kiss it awake.

Ray was that man—and he was in retreat. She watched as he continued down the path to the driveway, then turned, his gaze lingering on her, his eyes haunted.

He thought his love would doom her. Yet losing her chance for love with him felt like the worst sort of doom.

"WE'RE GOING TO have to put things on hold for a couple of days," he told DuChesne during his regular phone call. "She's leaving town."

"Leaving town?" DuChesne rasped. "What the hell is wrong with that girl?"

It occurred to Ray that Olivier DuChesne was one of the most self-centered people he'd ever encountered. Why *shouldn't* Hollis leave town for a couple of days? Why should DuChesne presume that she didn't have a full, active life?

"She's got some business to attend to," Ray said. He could have told DuChesne what her business was, but sheer orneriness prevented him. If his employer lacked the courtesy to inquire about his own daughter's career, Ray wasn't going to volunteer the information.

"Where is this business of hers?"

"New York City."

"Well, y'all had better go to New York City, too."

"Why? She'll be coming back in a few—"

"I don't want you letting her out of your sight."

"But...New York City?"

"I'm payin' your daily keep, Fargo. I'll pay for New York, too, if I have to. You aren't going to get her down to Serault Manor if you let her run off to the city and give you the slip."

Ray had been looking forward to a few days without her. Being near her tempted him too much, and in ways he wasn't used to. She wasn't just a woman to him, someone with whom he could share a few pleasures and then forget. She was...Hollis.

Hollis with the stormy eyes and the ivory skin. Hollis, whose photographs revealed her unique view of the world around her. Hollis, whose lips had fused with his and whose body had matched his, lured his, welcomed his.

Hollis, a woman he wanted as he hadn't wanted anyone since his wife's death. A woman he wanted so much, he had to drive her away to protect her.

"You can fly down to New York and take a room at the Plaza Hotel."

"The Plaza?"

"I've always stayed there during my sojourns to New York. It's a fine hotel."

"Isn't it one of those fancy high-priced places?"

"What do you care? I'm paying. I want y'all somewhere I know, so I can find you if I need you."

"All right," Ray conceded. "I'll go to New York."

DuChesne ended the call on a string of coughs. Ray lowered the receiver, sprawled out on the bed and let his head sink into the pillow. And tried to figure out how he was going to get through the next few days, how he was going to get through however many days it took for Hollis to change her mind about New Orleans or for DuChesne to give up and let Ray go home.

Closing his eyes, he pictured her in the thick twilight, seated beside him on the porch steps, listening as he told her about his wife. It was a subject he didn't discuss with anyone. Especially a woman he desired.

He hadn't told Hollis the story to earn her sympathy. He hadn't told her to shock her. He'd told her because he'd been desperate to put some distance between them.

But tonight, stretched out on the too-big bed in his motel room, he felt the distance narrowing again. His one chance to detach himself and regain his perspective had just been snatched from him.

He was going to New York.

And the damnedest thing was, one part of him was glad.

THE PLAZA HOTEL was as high-priced as Ray had suspected. Indeed, this entire jaunt—the last-minute airline ticket out of Albany, the cab fare from LaGuardia, a room reservation in one of New York's premium hotels—was going to cost DuChesne a small fortune.

Well, Ray thought as he unpacked the one suit he'd had the foresight to bring with him from New Orleans, it was DuChesne's fortune to waste.

He couldn't lose sight of the knowledge that Hollis was in the city right now. Probably at the gallery on Broome Street; he'd jotted down the address before returning her catalog yesterday. She couldn't be more than a few miles away from him—just as she'd never been more than a few miles away when they'd been in Vanderville.

In his imagination, she was never more than a few inches, a few moments away.

Ever since he'd left her house last night—ever since he'd first laid eyes on her—his mind had been filled with thoughts of her. His mind and his soul and his gut. He hadn't been able to taste the breakfast he'd wolfed down at Josie's that morning; all he could taste were Hollis's lips on his, her tongue meeting his. He had on a comfortable shirt and soft blue jeans, but he could feel only the pressure of her body moving against his, her hands groping at his chest, her hips seeking his.

In less than two hours he would be at her gallery show. He would be in the same room with her, watching her bask in her triumph. Her photographs would inspire applause, people would toast her and she would look radiant.

And he would want her.

Even though wanting her was the shortest route to disaster, even though if he became involved with her he would be sealing her fate, he would still want her.

THE CAB LET HIM OFF in front of the gallery at eight-fifteen, forty-five minutes after the doors officially opened. He hadn't cared about the fashionability of arriving late, but he'd wanted the gallery to be relatively crowded so he could slip in undetected. He didn't know what Hollis would do once she spotted him. But if the place was mobbed, she'd be less likely to throw a fit.

Bright light spilled through the glass door of the gallery. A line of perhaps half a dozen people stood on the sidewalk, awaiting entry. He joined the line, shoved his hair back from his forehead and fidgeted with the knot of his tie. He had no reason to be nervous.

Yes, he did—a bad reason. A foolish reason. A reason bred by his emotions rather than his intellect. He had to stifle it, tune it out, keep his mind on his job. Nervous wasn't going to get him what he wanted.

At last he made it inside the door. He strolled down a short, gray-walled corridor and into the main gallery. Ignoring the swarming people, the din of conversation and the trill of laughter, he scrutinized the prints adorning the walls. In their frames, illuminated by track lights, they looked fantastic.

He recognized one, of a fern surrounded by silver water. And another, of the amanita she'd photographed when he'd accompanied her into the woods. And others from the catalog, although they looked far more splendid in their enlarged renderings. Lord, he thought, she's really an artist.

Then he saw her at the far end of the gallery, enclosed within a cluster of adoring fans. She looked even more fantastic than her photographs.

She was dressed in a slim-fitting black sheath, with a strand of gold chain around her throat. Her hair was so dark, it almost seemed a part of the dress, and her eyes were enhanced with a touch of makeup. Her dress ended an inch above her knee, and her shoes had high heels. Through the forest of legs, Ray admired her sleek calves, her slender ankles and graceful insteps.

He let out a long, controlled breath and willed his body not to react to her. Lifting his gaze, he studied her face, her creamy skin, her swanlike neck, her lively smile.

She was more than he could fight with mere will. More statuesque, more radiant, more beautiful than he could talk himself out of desiring. This wasn't Hollis fuming about her father or weeping about her mother; it wasn't Hollis grimly relating the trials of her youth or grumbling about a less-than-perfect photographic print.

This was Hollis, a star, a princess, glorying in her success.

A waiter swept by carrying a tray of champagne. Ray absently took one of the fluted glasses, sipped from it, grimaced and set the glass down on the nearest table.

Voices surrounded him in a low murmur. Somewhere behind him a man pontificated on his theory that the photographs represented a metaphorical expression of Good and Evil. A slim blond woman with platinum hair edged up to him, slipped him a piece of paper with a phone number on it and disappeared into the crowd. He dropped the paper on the table next to his barely touched champagne.

Hollis remained at her post in the far corner, conversing with everyone who went over to pay homage to her. She looked so tall. So elegant. So composed.

Leaning against the wall beside a print of a burr enlarged to resemble one of those spiked maces the gladiators used to fight with, Ray folded his arms and watched as Hollis held court, as she tilted her head and considered a question, as she blushed with pleasure at a compliment, as she smiled and shook someone's hand. Her gaze circled the group around her, politely acknowledging each one.

Abruptly her smile faded and her eyes locked with Ray's. Through the thicket of guests, art connoisseurs and poseurs, she stared at Ray.

He held his breath, unsure of whether she would erupt in histrionics and demand his removal from the premises. Yesterday he'd begun a heated, unruly seduction in her carport, and then brought it to an abrupt halt with the warning that he carried the guilt of a woman's death on his back, in his soul. Even without their passionate encounter at her house last night, she resented him. As far as she was concerned, he was doing the devil's work—the devil being her father.

She couldn't possibly be pleased to see him here, casting his shadow across the brilliance of her show.

Yet slowly, painstakingly slowly, her lips curved in a smile.

Chapter Nine

At first she thought she'd hallucinated him. How could he be in Manhattan? Why was he there?

To attend her show's opening, of course. He'd come to check it out. He'd come out of curiosity.

Or else he'd come because he couldn't stay away.

"Ms. Griffin!" someone shouted into her left ear. "I've just got to tell you, that shot of the dead leaves..."

Tearing her gaze from Ray, she presented the fellow on her left with a polite smile. She listened patiently as he told her about how much the photo reminded him of the piles of dead leaves he used to jump in as a child, and thanked him for his kind words. And all the while her heart was racing, her pulse thundering in her ears. Ray was in New York, in this gallery, seeing the same prints and lights and people as she, breathing the same air.

When at last the man at her elbow stopped yammering about dead leaves, she glanced toward where she'd seen Ray a moment ago. He was gone. She suffered a stab of panic. Maybe she *had* hallucinated him. Maybe she'd been thinking about him so much, she'd only imagined seeing him. Maybe the sight of him was only an empty hope conjured by her overactive imagination.

For it was an empty hope. No matter how much she wanted Ray—and how much he wanted her—nothing was going to come of it. She had to stop dreaming about him, obsessing on him, wishing things were different, wishing—

There he was again. She spotted him standing amid a cluster of wealthy-looking art patrons. He looked too real to be a mirage. His eyes were too haunting, his lips too sensual, his body too tall and firm in his rumpled gray suit and loosened tie.

Someone was yammering at her again, this time in praise of one of the amanita photos. She remembered to nod and mumble her thanks, but her voice was thick, her vision riveted to Ray. Unlike most of the people in the room, he wasn't holding a champagne glass, and he didn't seem to know what to do with his hands. He dug one into his trouser pocket, raked the other through his thick dark hair, then tapped his fingers against the nearest table. He seemed tense.

She wanted to go over to him. She wanted to take his restless hands in hers and tell him to stop worrying, to stop trying to protect her, to forget everything that waited for him in Louisiana—her father, his memories, all of it—and just *be* with her throughout the show, experience it with her, stand by her. She took a step toward him, but the throng around her closed ranks, someone started speaking about a portrait of pine needles, and when she looked toward Ray, he was gone.

She knew she hadn't imagined him. She felt his presence even if she couldn't see him, felt it in the constant drumming of her pulse, the languid heat touring the length of her spine, the strange shortness of breath that turned her words into sighs.

After a minute she located him conversing with a stunning six-foot-tall woman as slim and chiseled as a fashion model. As if he could feel Hollis's gaze on him, he turned. His smile was guarded, but his eyes hid nothing. They were dark, smoldering, sending out a message she was afraid to interpret. Her pulse drummed faster, her body grew warmer.

Someone handed her a glass of champagne, and she drank it. The gallery owner pulled her aside to report that she'd already received a few orders, that a critic from the *New York Times* had arrived and the buzz around the gallery was that Hollis Griffin was a hit. "You're moving into the pantheon, honey," Suzanne confided proudly. "You're a star. By the way, who's that interesting-looking guy with the Southern accent?"

"He's...a friend," Hollis mumbled, aware that the word bore no relation to what Ray was.

"Half the women here have come on to him, and he keeps brushing them off. Is he gay?"

Recalling last night's kisses, the heat of his hands against her skin, the way he'd swelled and pressed against her, Hollis choked on a laugh. "No, he's not."

"Then he must be in love with someone."

"Maybe." Hollis swallowed another anxious laugh. She shifted her gaze, and it unerringly found him. He was watching her, his smile subtle, mysterious. She wanted to know what he was thinking, what his smile was telling her. She wanted to march over to him and ask him. Or touch him. Or pull him to herself the way she had in the carport, and not let him run away. It was a yearning she'd never known before. But she wasn't imagining it any more than she was imagining the fact that he was standing in this room.

By ten o'clock the crowd began to thin. At long last Ray approached her. "So, darlin', how does fame suit you?"

Standing close to him set her nervous system on high alert. Fame had nothing to do with what she was feeling right now. Once again, Ray eclipsed the world around her, blocking out thoughts of her show, her success, her career.

Her hands grew icy; her heartbeat raced. She concealed her uneasiness by joking, "Fame I could take or leave. It's the adulation I really like."

"Whatever turns you on."

You, she almost blurted out. *You turn me on.* "Why are you here, Ray?" She stared into his eyes and hoped that he would be as honest with her now as he'd always been.

He glanced away and then back at her, a wistful grin shaping his lips. "Your father told me to come."

He might as well have kicked her in the stomach. She had been wrestling with her passions all evening; she'd been reveling in his having traveled such a great distance to be with her. She had been fantasizing that her triumph at the gallery would be surpassed by other triumphs, the excitement of knowing Ray had vanquished his grief and come to her. She had spent the past two hours drowning in her awareness of Ray Fargo.

And the only reason he had come was that he was under orders from the heartless, soulless, filthy-rich scoundrel who'd fathered her.

"Well," she muttered, wondering if Ray could hear the hurt in her tone. "Sorry you had to make the trip." She busied herself pulling off her shoes. Her feet weren't as sore as her heart, but she could do something to alleviate them. Alleviating the pain in her heart seemed impossible.

Balanced on one foot, she teetered. He caught her arm and held her upright. His chivalrous touch sent a flurry of sensation through her, and she hated herself for reacting to him when he'd all but told her he didn't give a damn about her.

Regaining her balance, she yanked her arm free and glared at him. His hesitant smile thawed her anger.

"It's true I didn't want to come," he conceded. "I knew if I did I would never be able to leave your side."

She couldn't let herself take his compliment to heart. Delta silt, that was all it was. "You managed to stay far away from my side," she pointed out. "You've been here for hours, and this is the first time you've spoken to me."

"I didn't want to interfere with all that adulation," he said, still smiling a smile that sent ripples of unwelcome longing through her. "I knew everyone would leave sooner or later, and then we'd talk."

"Go ahead, then," she said brusquely. "Talk."

"You're magnificent."

Coming from him, it didn't sound anything like the fawning praise she'd received all evening. "Oh, I'm sure I am," she scoffed. "But of course it doesn't matter how magnificent I am, or what we feel for each other. We have to keep our distance. You're too dangerous."

"Don't say it," he whispered. His hand was still on her arm, his fingers firm but gentle. "I know it's true, but I don't want to think about it."

"It's not true," she argued. "It's just some silly superstition—"

"No, darlin'. It's true. But if I accept it I'll have to walk away from you again. And I don't think I'm strong enough to do that."

She peered up into his troubled brown eyes. "I think you're strong enough *not* to walk away," she murmured, aware that his longing matched hers, exceeded it, submerged his fears and misgivings, supplanted them.

She raised her head as he lowered his, and their lips met in a brief, intense reunion. "God forgive me," he whispered, then brushed his lips over hers again. "I want to spend the night with you."

She struggled to remain lucid. "I'll be spending the night driving back to Vanderville."

"Stay with me. I took a hotel room for the night."

Her heart lurched. "A hotel room?"

"Right here in the city. We'll go back to Vanderville tomorrow."

"What about..." Her voice dissolved into a sigh as he grazed her brow with his lips. "What about my father?"

"What about him? Tonight is between you and me, Hollis. He has nothing to do with it."

What was between her and Ray was desire. Need. Love. Her father and Ray's wife were irrelevant. The only danger they faced was the danger of any two people about to cross the line, about to become lovers.

If Ray could be brave enough to face that danger, so could Hollis. "Yes," she whispered. "I'll stay with you."

HER KNEES FELT WEAK, and it had nothing to do with her high heels. Awed by the lavish decor of the Plaza's lobby, the beveled mirrors and crystal fixtures, the deep carpet and the marble counters bedecked with fresh flowers, she held Ray's arm and willed herself not to panic.

As they rode the elevator upstairs, she couldn't bear to let go of him. She wanted to absorb his warmth, his strong male essence. She wanted to be so close to him, no one would know where she ended and he began.

The elevator stopped on an upper floor. They strolled down the hall to his room. And then he shut the door and locked it, and she fell into his arms.

He kissed her—a deep, devouring kiss. His tongue danced with hers, dueled with it, gave and took and conquered her. He flattened his hands against her back, one between her shoulder blades and one below her waist, and guided her hips and breasts against him. She gasped as he pressed between her thighs, as he moved against her and groaned and gathered her even more snugly to himself.

She slid her hands under his jacket. He stopped kissing her long enough to let her shove the jacket off his shoulders. As it dropped to the floor, he yanked open the knot of his tie, and she tore at the buttons of his shirt until they were undone. Reaching inside the shirt, she skimmed her fingers over the hot skin of his chest, the spear of hair darting from his nipples to his belly, the smooth, taut surface of his abdomen. When she reached the edge of his trousers, his hips surged reflexively.

The bulge of his arousal stunned her. How she wanted to satisfy him, satisfy him so well he forgot all about his wife forever. It was an unforgivable thought, greedy and fraught with a love Hollis had no right to feel. Ray didn't love her. His life was far away, somewhere where she didn't belong. She couldn't let herself love him.

She heard a faint moan, arousal mixed with despair. Ray drew back and wrestled with his breath for a minute. "What is it?" he asked, his voice uneven.

"Nerves, I guess." Feeling a blush heat her cheeks, she turned away. She couldn't bear for him to see the love she knew was blazing in her eyes. He was so anxious to protect her, he might bring everything to a halt if he knew she loved him.

Worse, he might *not* bring everything to a halt. He might not care about breaking her heart.

He moved behind her and molded his hands to her shoulders. He dug his thumbs into the knot of tension at the base of her skull, and then brushed his lips against the crown of her head. "Don't be scared," he said.

"I'm not scared." She sounded terrified.

"I'll make it sweet for you, so sweet. . . ."

He browsed down to her earlobe, lifted her hair and kissed the nape of her neck. Slowly, unable to resist his soothing kisses, she leaned back against him. He circled her with his arms, fondled her breasts, then drew his hands down the front of her dress to her hips, her thighs.

Gathering up the black crepe, he lifted the dress as high as her waist. He brought one hand back down, over her panty hose and between her legs. His touch sent a wave of heat deep into her.

"Trust me, Hollis," he murmured, moving his hand again, pressing, cupping, stroking her through the nylon. "Let me love you.... Yes." He sighed as her instincts took over. She angled her hips, arching against his fingers as he seduced her with his deft caresses. She felt herself softening, melting, liquefying as he pulled her against him and ran his fingers along her inner thighs.

She almost protested when he let go of her, but he'd done so only to unzip her dress. She closed her eyes and shivered as his hands glided across her back, unfastening her bra, easing her slip down her legs, peeling off her nylons. Her skin felt overly sensitized, her veins too full, her nerves strung taut. Every inch of her body quivered with expectation.

She ought to be doing something for him, she thought—touching him, arousing him. Yet she was in a trance, too attuned to the pleasures he was kindling within her to remember what she was supposed to do. When she was completely undressed, he turned her in his arms and gazed down at her. "I can't believe how beautiful you are," he said, his tone ragged, his eyes glazed with longing. She realized that she was doing something for him simply by standing naked before him.

She laughed softly. "Don't pour on the flattery."

"This isn't silt, woman. Just the truth." His gaze never leaving her, he shed his shirt, yanked open his belt, shucked his trousers.

She allowed herself to study him as he studied her. He was the beautiful one, she thought, admiring the lean contours of his body, the powerful breadth of his shoulders and the narrowness of his hips, the defined muscles of his thighs and calves, the swell of his aroused flesh curving up toward his stomach.

Hesitantly she reached out and ran her finger along his swollen length. He stood motionless, holding his breath. She felt the strain, the heat, the steel hardness of him, and a dark tremor coursed through her.

He brought her to the bed, laid her across it and then stretched out beside her. Bowing, he kissed her, nibbled her lips, caught her lower lip between his teeth, curled his tongue around hers. He kissed her so thoroughly, she could scarcely keep track of his hand journeying from her shoulders to her breasts and teasing her nipples until they were taut and aching. The ache spread downward as his hand moved lower, massaging her midriff, circling her belly, then sliding into the downy hair between her legs.

Her body jerked as he found her, but he stilled her with another consuming kiss. Unable to cry out, she gripped his shoulders and held him to her, kissing him in return, filling his mouth with a plaintive moan as he rubbed his fingers against her damp, hot flesh, sending wave after wave of burning need into her. It hurt, it felt too good, it tormented her. She wanted him to stop. She wanted him to carry her further, to take her where she'd never been before. She wanted release. She wanted eternity.

She wanted Ray.

What she had was his hand, luring her closer and closer to that release, that eternity. She hovered on the edge of something, balanced, reaching... And then she plunged, tumbling down through layers of sensation, seething, searing pulses of it. She clung to him, afraid that the glorious storm inside her would tear her from him, from everything she knew. Only he could catch her and break her fall before she crashed into a million pieces.

A low moan scraped across her throat, a raw sound of shock and delight. She opened her eyes and her vision filled with him, with his golden-brown eyes and his enigmatic smile. If anything was better than what she'd just experienced, it was emerging to discover herself in his arms.

"How are you doing?" he asked.

She was doing fine. Better than fine. But there was more, she knew. There was Ray.

She answered his question by reaching up to touch his face, the firm edge of his jaw, the surprisingly silky texture of his hair. She traced the width of his shoulders, the supple surface of his chest, the slope of his waist. The dense hair below his abdomen, the hard shaft of his arousal.

She touched him, stroked him, curved her palm around him until he closed his eyes and shuddered. Pushing her hands away, he rose fully onto her and nudged her legs apart.

"Stay with me," he whispered.

She nodded, trusting him, loving him.

With a powerful thrust he penetrated her, filling not just her body but her mind, her soul. He was fierce, possessive, moving inside her with savage grace, stirring embers that had not yet died.

She absorbed every sensory detail: the scent of his soap and his clean, male sweat, the feel of his muscular weight, the rasp of his breath, the salty taste of his skin as she kissed his cheek and his jaw. She kept her eyes open, not wanting to miss the magnificent sight of his face, his gaze uniting with hers as his body did, his hair falling across his brow, his lips parted and ready for another kiss.

She tightened her arms around him, pulling herself against him. He groaned and lifted her legs higher around his waist. His chest rubbed sensuously against her breasts as he surged deeper, farther, setting off more sparks, stoking the fire inside her. His mouth moved against her temple, her brow. "You feel so good, so good...."

His hips moved in an inexorable rhythm. His lips streaked over her damp cheeks. His hand glided down her side, pausing to squeeze her breast, to round her bottom, to skim her thigh. He pulled her legs higher yet, then wedged his hand between his body and hers. At his touch she exploded, her body bucking, her hands fisting against his back as a fresh burst of sensation tore through her.

She cried out, certain that this time she wouldn't survive. Ray couldn't save her; he was lost in his own splendid climax. His body wrenched inside her; he gasped, then groaned and sank onto her, deep into her, seeking shelter as he sheltered her, holding on to her as desperately as she held on to him.

After a long while, Hollis felt her mind clear. She had survived, after all. So had Ray. He lay heavily on top of her, his breath unusually deep, his hand twining through the hair behind her ear.

"Am I crushing you?" he asked.

"Yes." But she closed her arms around him when he tried to raise himself. "I didn't say I minded," she pointed out.

He laughed. His chest vibrated against her, and she laughed, too. He pushed against her arms, and his strength forced her to loosen her embrace. Propping himself up, he smiled down into her face. "In my wildest fantasies, Hollis, I can't imagine anything more exciting than having you underneath me getting crushed—except maybe having you on top of me, doing the crushing. We'll have to try that next time."

The prospect of a next time sent a shimmering spasm of warmth through her. "This isn't a fantasy," she said, needing to convince herself as much as him.

His smile expanded, illuminating his eyes. "Just a small miracle, right?"

A miracle, yes—but not small.

Ray *did* love her. Maybe not the way she did, maybe not forever after. But he couldn't have given so much of himself if he didn't love her. She'd seen it, felt it, heard it in his groan of surrender. He loved her.

His love liberated her. The past was what it was—past. Gone. Over and done with. She had no more use for hatred, resentment, bitterness. Her heart swelled with love, for the world, for everything and everyone in it, for Ray. Especially for Ray.

Gazing up at him, she saw her love reflected in his bright, dazzling eyes. Gone were the shadows, gone was the grief. Perhaps she had liberated Ray the way he'd liberated her. Perhaps he, too, had set down his burdens and freed himself to share in the love that Hollis had found in his arms.

"If I had my camera right now, I'd want to photograph you," she murmured, reveling in the striking lines and angles of his face.

"Do I remind you of a mushroom?"

She laughed again. It felt wonderful to laugh with Ray.

"Or is it that you just want a shot of me in my birthday suit, for blackmailing purposes?"

"That's more up your alley, Mr. Private Eye."

"Well, now that you mention it, I wouldn't mind a few nude shots of you. I'd put one on my desk, so I'd have something to keep my mind occupied when business is slow."

"Why don't you just buy one of those girlie calendars?"

"They don't have you in them." He rolled off her, arranging himself on his side and arranging her comfortably in his arms. "I'm very particular about those kinds of photos. Not just anyone will do."

She twined her fingers through the hair on his chest, smiling when her light caress prompted a moan from him. She lowered her gaze to his chest, suddenly too shy to look him squarely in the eye when she said, "I'd like to go to New Orleans with you."

He clamped one hand over hers so she couldn't stroke him, and used his other to tilt her face up to his. "You mean, to be with me?" he asked, looking directly into her eyes.

She met his gaze without wavering. "That would be nice, Ray. But that wasn't what I meant."

"Your father."

She nodded. *My father,* she thought, amazed that she could think of Olivier DuChesne without rancor or fury. Amazed that she could embrace the thought of him as *my father.*

A delicate tendril of love sprouted inside her, separate from the lush blossoming of love she harbored for Ray. This was something different, something born of forgiveness, of acceptance. Something that could grow only in a heart no longer locked in bitterness.

"Take me there," she said. "I want to meet him."

Chapter Ten

"I'm here! I'm actually in New Orleans!"

"You actually are," Ray agreed, doing his best to ignore the vague dread that had been gnawing at him ever since he and Hollis had boarded the plane in Albany a few hours—a lifetime—ago.

Should he have brought her to Olivier DuChesne? Was the old man going to dash her hopes and wound her ego? What if she took one look at the father she'd been crying for all her life, sometimes without even realizing that he was what she was crying for, and all her bitterness came back? What if she wound up the worse for having met him?

She'd made love with Ray, after all. She'd broken through his defenses and made him care about her. Bad luck was bound to befall her the way it had befallen the last woman who'd loved him.

Forget about it, he told himself. *You've done your job. Take the money and run.*

Twenty-five thousand dollars. Over the past few days, during which he'd gone back to Vanderville with Hollis, shared her joy at the success of her gallery show and helped her prepare for her sojourn to New

Orleans, a tiny, unsentimental, vicious little whisper echoed in the back of his skull. *She's a job. A case. Don't get involved. Just deliver her to Serault Manor, collect your bounty and move on.*

That line of thought pained him. Yet, if he detoured from it, he wound up traveling in an even more dangerous direction. *You care about Hollis. You care about her a lot.*

And if you care about her, she's doomed.

It was better if he didn't care at all. For her sake even more than his own.

The plane rolled to a stop by the terminal. Ray turned to find Hollis gazing around her, looking dazed but happy. She twisted in her seat until she was facing him, and erupted in a spontaneous musical laugh. When she curled her hand around his wrist, he had to muster all his self-control not to grab her and hang on tight.

"I feel as if I've been reborn," she said, then laughed again.

He clamped his mouth shut to keep from squelching her enthusiasm. If she wanted to feel reborn, who was he to say otherwise?

They made their way down the aisle and into the terminal. "I'm in New Orleans!" she exclaimed, sounding ecstatic.

Unfortunately, the more jubilant Hollis acted, the more gloomy he felt. He had to smother the impulse to drag her to a ticket counter and buy her a ticket back to Albany, shouting, "Go, before it's too late."

Too late for what? He wished he knew.

They headed down the corridor to the baggage-claim area, Hollis practically skipping and Ray trudging. He tried to shake off his growing sense of foreboding. So help him, if anything happened to Hollis, anything at all...

The only thing that was going to happen to her was that she was going to meet the family she'd never known. She was going to become acquainted with her half brother and half sister, and she was going to make peace with her father before it was too late. And when DuChesne died, she was probably going to find herself a very rich heiress.

And Ray would pocket his fee—plus twenty-five thousand dollars—and get on with his life.

He wished things could be different. The few nights he'd spent with Hollis had been spectacular. When he kissed her breasts and heard her sweet sighs, when she twined her fingers through his hair and held his mouth to hers, when she wrapped those long, long legs of hers around him and held him deep inside her, when he felt her cresting around him...

He hadn't known sex could be so good. It had never been before. Maybe it would never be again.

But that didn't matter. He couldn't stay with her. She was in the process of being reborn, as she herself had put it, and the kindest thing he could do was get out of her way.

Their suitcases tumbled down the chute, and Ray lifted them from the carousel. "How would you like to handle this?" he asked, laboring to keep his voice devoid of emotion. "Do you want to rest up tonight and pay a call on Serault Manor tomorrow morning?"

"Oh, no—I want to go there right now. It's only three o'clock in the afternoon. You told my father we were flying in today. He won't mind my coming straight from the airport, will he?"

"Darlin', he's been so eager to meet you, I don't think he'd mind if you rang his bell at midnight. Let's go see if my car forgives me for leaving it stranded for so long."

After a minor, whiny protest, the car started. It was old but reliable, a nondescript Ford well suited to Ray's occasional surveillance jobs because it didn't call attention to itself.

The highway into town was no more picturesque than any other highway out of any other airport. But Hollis gaped at the sights. "Look at the palm trees!" she exclaimed. "And those pastel stucco buildings. This place is like the tropics."

"Hollis..." He didn't know why he felt obligated to warn her, but he did.

She shifted in her seat to gaze at him, and when he glanced away from the road, he saw her dazzling smile. The sight nearly broke his heart.

"Yes?" she prompted him after a prolonged silence.

He let out a breath he hadn't realized he was holding. "I've brought families together before, Hollis. I've found missing persons, adoptees and birth mothers and all that. I've witnessed some of these reunions. People have such high expectations, but it doesn't always work out happily ever after."

She did him the favor of looking solemn. "I know that, Ray. I'm prepared for the worst."

"It doesn't look that way to me."

"Well, I am. Olivier DuChesne can't be more of a bastard than I've always thought he was. At least I'll be able to say hello to him and find out about my genetic background. And maybe by meeting him, I'll be able to understand my mother better. That's important to me."

"Of course it's important," Ray conceded, wishing he could do a better job at whatever the hell it was he was trying to accomplish during the short drive into town.

"Besides," she continued, her serene smile returning, "this is my hometown. The place where I was born. New Orleans." She whispered the words reverently. "My roots are here. Maybe this is where I belong." Her smile grew bashful when she added, "And of course, *you're* here, too."

He ground his teeth together and locked his gaze on the road. He wanted to promise that he would keep her with him forever. But he'd made that promise to another woman, and "forever" had wound up lasting less than five years.

He couldn't bring himself to say *Yes, Hollis, I'm here for you.* Nor could he bring himself to say she should forget about him. He could only hope that she would be welcomed into the bosom of the DuChesne family, and they would shower her with so much love she would no longer need Ray.

"Look! There's the Superdome!" Her eyes widened with excitement. Ray's narrowed with trepidation. They had reached the exit and were within minutes of Serault Manor.

He ought to be thrilled that she was so cheerful. He'd certainly worked long and hard to get her to this place. Yet the dark pulse of doom continued to pound inside his head.

"This is called the Garden District," he said, navigating through the lushly landscaped neighborhood of huge, old residences. Hollis oohed and aahed over some of the more impressive houses. Ray wondered what she would think when she saw her father's home, which made even the fancier domiciles lining the road look like mere shacks in comparison.

He reached the six-foot-high, wrought-iron gate that marked the foot of the driveway leading between two lesser estates to the unseen mansion where Olivier DuChesne lived. Turning onto the drive, he rolled down his window, pressed a button and stared into the camera affixed to one of the brick pillars flanking the gate.

Through the speaker, he heard the butler's voice. "Yes?"

"It's Ray Fargo. I've got Mr. DuChesne's daughter with me."

"Very well."

The speaker emitted a spray of static, and the gates swung inward to admit Ray's car.

Hollis sat quietly beside Ray, her ebullience fading, replaced by a more reflective mood. While she'd been enraptured by the scenery earlier, now she seemed hardly to notice the groomed magnolia trees, the palmettos and bougainvillea lining the brick drive, the lush lawns rolling out on either side, the rich, damp perfume of a September afternoon in New Orleans. At last, she was beginning to suffer from nerves.

He ought to say something to comfort her, but he couldn't. He'd been honest with her from the start; he wasn't about to start lying now. And he couldn't help but feel that any words of comfort would be a lie.

Up ahead loomed the rococo palace with its magisterial entry, its semicircular portico, its massive Corinthian pillars, its huge, heavily draped leaded-glass windows. Hollis drew in a quick, sharp breath as the reality of her father's wealth sank in.

"Good Lord. Is this his house?"

"Serault Manor. It's been in his family—or should I say, in *your* family—since the early nineteenth century."

"Look at it." She sounded appropriately awed, her tone breathy. She didn't wait for Ray to open her door, but stepped out of the car and tilted her head back to stare at the massive slate roof sloping up above the third-story windows, the elaborate masonry of the walls, the porch vast enough to stage a Wagnerian opera, the front door a slab of carved mahogany ten feet tall and five feet wide, flanked by beveled crystal sidelights. "Somebody actually *lives* here?"

"Your father does. And I reckon you'll be living here with him for the next few days."

She shook her head. Ray wondered whether she was comparing the mansion to the drab dwellings she had called "home" as a child. If her father had done right by her mother, Hollis would have grown up in these sumptuous surroundings, instead.

"I've been inside only once," Ray told her, pulling her suitcase from the trunk. "I recall the interior being kind of intimidating. Like a museum."

"I can handle it."

He hoped she could.

They sauntered along the slate path and up the eight marble steps to the porch. "Do you have those papers I told you to bring?" he asked.

"In that pocket." She pointed to a zippered compartment on her suitcase. Ray opened it and pulled out the envelope containing her birth certificate and other documents that positively identified her as Olivier DuChesne's daughter. DuChesne had insisted on the documentation. He wanted to be sure he was not welcoming an imposter into his family.

Ray rang the bell. After a moment, the towering door inched open to reveal the butler. Ray had met him when he'd visited the house. The butler stood as tall as Ray but was slighter in build. His navy blazer hung from bony shoulders; his striped gray trousers bloused around his legs. His face reminded Ray of a vulture's, his nose beaklike and his neck skeletal.

"Mr. Fargo," he said in that affected voice of his.

"This is Hollis Griffin. Mr. DuChesne's daughter."

Hollis gave the man a winsome smile. He inspected her, then sniffed haughtily. "Have you brought proof?"

Not the warmest greeting in the world. Hollis appeared unfazed, though. She nodded to Ray, who handed the documents to the butler.

He pulled out her driver's license and compared the photograph on it with the face of the woman before him. Then he read the birth certificate and the baptismal certificate. He sniffed again.

"Very well." He stuffed the papers back into the envelope, placed his fingers under Hollis's elbow, and drew her over the thick doorsill and into the foyer. She craned her neck to view the ornate wall coverings, the intricate sconces, the circular staircase rising to an open second-floor hallway, and then up farther, to the third floor. The domed ceiling was painted with fat-cheeked cherubs reveling among cotton-puff clouds.

Turning, she sent Ray an astonished look.

He wanted to join her in the entry. Somehow he couldn't shake the sense that they belonged on the same side of the threshold.

The butler lifted her suitcase from the porch and set it down on the tiled floor inside the door. Then he reached into an inner pocket of his blazer and pulled out another envelope, this one bulging. Hollis eyed the envelope curiously.

Ray eyed it suspiciously. His instincts told him he wasn't going to like what was about to happen.

The butler lifted the envelope's flap and pulled out a thick wad of currency. "Twenty-five thousand dollars," he said in his imperious accent. "Would you care to count it?"

"No. I thought—" Ray glanced at Hollis. Her gaze remained on the envelope for an instant longer, then rose to him. She looked confused, and then gradually horrified. Ray hastily returned his gaze to the butler. "I was planning to send a bill," he said.

"You may invoice Mr. DuChesne and itemize your expenses. This is your bonus, as agreed upon when you accepted Mr. DuChesne's business. The terms were that if you delivered Mr. DuChesne's daughter—"

"I remember the terms," Ray muttered, risking another glimpse at Hollis. She stared at him in blatant anger.

"You agreed to those terms, Mr. Fargo. You were quite pleased with them. Now kindly take your money and go."

Ray stared at the envelope and wondered what the butler would do if he refused to take it. He *couldn't* take it, not with Hollis watching him, assuming the worst and hating him for it. Even without Hollis watching him he'd be reluctant. A cash payment didn't sit well with him.

The butler extended the envelope toward him. "You may go now," he repeated.

"I'd like to talk to Mr. DuChesne first," Ray demanded.

"That won't be possible. He's feeling quite ill. He's receiving no visitors at the moment."

Ray gestured toward the envelope in the butler's outstretched hand. "I can't accept this."

"You agreed to his terms. Take it and go."

Ray turned helplessly to Hollis. Her eyes met his for one brief, blazing instant. He saw resentment in them, shock, fury. A sheen of tears. Before he could speak—before he could breach the invisible divider separating him on the porch from her in the foyer—she turned away from him and hugged her arms to herself. She was holding herself in, embracing herself the way she'd once embraced Ray. She was closing him off.

He considered his options. He could appeal to her for understanding. He could tell her the money was irrelevant, and he'd brought her to New Orleans only because he believed it was the best thing for her.

She would never believe that. He wasn't sure he would believe it himself.

If he refused the money, she'd think him a jackass as well as a hypocrite. If he took the money and left, as the butler clearly expected him to do, perhaps she would be safe from whatever danger Ray might have brought down on her. Taking the money would mean he and Hollis were no longer lovers, and would never be lovers again. It would buy him a way out of a relationship he shouldn't have entered in the first place, and it would give her an excuse not to pine for him. It would offer them a nice, clean break.

A nice *dirty* break, he amended.

He leaned across the threshold and touched her shoulder. She spun around, and he saw the torment in her hurricane-dark eyes. She no longer loathed Olivier DuChesne. But she loathed Ray Fargo.

Take it and go. The butler's voice resounded inside him. Calm, firm, categorical. No room for negotiations or explanations, no space for special pleading. *Take it and go.*

Ray took the envelope and went.

NOT UNTIL SHE HEARD the sound of the heavy wood door click shut did Hollis resume breathing. She'd had to hold herself perfectly still. If she allowed herself to move at all, she would have sprung at Ray with fists flying.

How could he? How could he have taken that money in exchange for her? She felt like chattel, a piece of furniture, a high-priced slave. *How could he?*

The answer was obvious—and even more painful than the question. He had *always* intended to take the money. He had *always* intended to sell her to her father. He had done whatever he'd had to do to get his hands on that filthy wad of cash: hike into the woods after her, help her with her prints, feed her, follow her to New York, make love to her.

Make her love him.

For money. He'd done it all for an envelope stuffed with high-denomination bills.

It was no consolation to remind herself that he was a professional, and as such he deserved to be paid for his labor. The way the man in the navy blazer had handed him the envelope right in front of her, as if he were purchasing her....Professionals didn't operate that way.

A strange chill gathered around her. She was trapped in a baroque Southern castle with a strange, hawklike man and those weird frescoes of pudgy angels seemingly miles above her head, and Ray had been bought off. He was no longer a part of this. Whatever occurred next, she had to face it on her own.

Her father. That was what was going to occur next: a meeting with her father.

"I will take you to your room. Minnie will help you to unpack."

"Minnie?" Her half sister, she hoped. Or her stepmother.

"The maid."

"I'd like to see my father," she declared, forcing herself to sound assertive.

"That will not be possible," the gaunt man said. "He's feeling much too poorly this afternoon." The butler led the way to the stairs and started up them, moving at an uncannily even pace. "Would you like me to send up some ice coffee?"

"I'd prefer hot tea," she said. Her stomach twisted with nerves; perhaps some tea would help settle it.

By the time she'd hiked the twenty-five stairs to the second floor, she was feeling queasy. The ornate ambiance of the rotunda-like foyer cloyed. Everything was carved or gilded; the wall sconces were filigreed brass with etched crystals hanging from them; the rug ribboning the center of the stairs featured a dizzying pattern of bloodred roses and snaking vines.

At the top of the curving flight the man turned left down a broad hallway. Hollis followed, wondering behind which closed door her father might be, or her other long-lost relatives. She hoped she would meet them soon. She was feeling more alone than ever before. It was bad enough to lose your mother because of a terrible accident. Far worse was to lose a lover because he'd betrayed you.

She had never felt so alone in all her life.

Chin up, she exhorted herself. *Stiff upper lip.* She was at Serault Manor and she might as well make the best of it. In a few days, she could return to Vanderville, her camera and her career. In the solitude of her house, in the seclusion of her basement workrooms or the tranquility of the woods, she could fall apart.

After an extremely long walk, the man pushed open a door, entered the room and set down her bag. "I shall have Minnie bring you some tea," he said, gesturing her inside and then leaving.

She looked around. The room was huge, with a pale green carpet, green-and-peach-hued wallpaper, elaborate, slightly dusty cornices, a massive marble fireplace—which showed no sign of recent use—and the furnishings she expected to find in a bedroom, although everything was proportioned to fill the large room. The triple dresser, armoire, desk and easy chair were all of French Provincial design. The bed was a queen-size four-poster.

She crossed to the French doors and tugged on the brass handle. The doors opened onto a tiny balcony that overlooked a small garden patio surrounded by dense green shrubs pruned into a hedge of spheres.

Tears burned her eyes, but she blinked them away and rested her hands on the wrought-iron railing. The hell with Ray Fargo. The hell with his tragic past and his sorrowful eyes. The hell with his lips, his hands, his body. His smile, his sexy drawl, his phony concern for her. She didn't need him.

A single tear escaped, slid down her cheek and dripped from her chin. She imagined it plunging to the patio far, far below her.

"Miz Hollis?" a voice called to her from the room.

She turned. A thin, drawn woman with matted gray hair and a pinched look about her was setting down a silver tea service on the desk.

Hollis took a deep breath, then reentered the room. She wasn't used to valets and maids, silver service and deluxe accommodations. But Ray's duplicity had devastated her so completely, an overly elegant room and a pair of servants couldn't addle her.

"Lowery said y'all wanted some tea," the maid drawled, looking past Hollis at the afternoon light spilling in through the window. "Y'all drink some while I unpack your things."

"You don't have to do that," Hollis said, but the maid had already hoisted Hollis's bag onto the bed and was opening it. Hollis decided not to fight her about it. She really wanted a cup of tea more than she wanted to unpack.

She poured some from the silver pot into a delicate cup. Steam rose from it, and she blew on it before sipping. It was like no tea she'd ever had before, almost sour, with a biting aftertaste.

"What kind of tea is this?" she asked, trying not to grimace.

"It's an herbal blend."

"Lowery—is that the name of the man who brought me upstairs?"

"Yes."

"And you're Minnie?"

"Yes." The skinny woman bustled about the room, placing articles of clothing in the armoire and the dresser, carrying Hollis's toiletries bag into the adjacent bathroom.

Hollis waited until Minnie returned before asking, "Can you take me to my father?"

"Not today, Miz Hollis. He's mightily ill."

Hollis forced down another sip of tea. "How about Mrs. DuChesne? I'd like to see her."

Minnie stopped and frowned at Hollis, although once again her eyes seemed to focus on something just behind Hollis. "Miz DuChesne isn't here."

"She isn't?"

"She and the twins are on a Mediterranean cruise. They won't be back for a month at least."

Hollis sank onto the stiff-backed desk chair and struggled to hang on to her composure. She had been eager to meet her half siblings. She had thought she would be joining a real, true family.

But now three of that family's members were on a cruise a hemisphere away, and the fourth member was too sick to receive his guest. Why had he insisted on Hollis's coming here? Why had he paid Ray all that money just to have her sit in a humongous room overlooking a cute little garden?

"I don't understand," she murmured.

Minnie smiled, but since she refused to look at Hollis, her smile offered cold comfort. "Y'all have some tea now," she said, snapping shut the suitcase and storing it in the armoire. "Dinner's at six."

Before Hollis could question her further, the mousy gray-haired maid was gone.

"HELLO, EVALINE," Ray growled at his secretary as he entered the front room of the second-floor office on Royal Street.

His secretary glanced up from her computer monitor and smiled hesitantly. "Welcome back," she said. "Y'all want your messages?"

"Later."

"How was the flight?"

"Fine," he said, barreling past her and into his own office. He slammed the door so hard, a shower of dust rained down from the transom. Fortunately, Evaline Hammond, the finest secretary in the entire state of Louisiana, would know better than to interrogate him about his foul mood.

He slumped in his leather swivel chair, yanked off his blazer and flung it across the room. Then he thought about the envelope that he'd left in his safe-deposit box at the bank on his way to the French Quarter.

He couldn't deposit twenty-five thousand dollars in cash, not without the bank's filling out a stack of forms. Federal law required banks to report any large cash deposits, since such cash deposits frequently resulted from illegal drug sales.

Besides, if Ray had deposited the cash into his business account, it would be tantamount to accepting it. And he wasn't ready to do that.

Something didn't feel right about his few minutes at Serault Manor. It had nothing to do with Hollis; he was sure she would be fine. In fact, with Ray out of her life—which was evidently the way she wanted it, if her hostile expression was any indication—she was probably better off.

No, he wasn't worried about her. He wasn't feeling bad about the malice he'd seen in her too-expressive eyes. He wasn't brooding over the rather grim prospect of never again nibbling that full lower lip of hers, never feeling her hands clawing at his back, never feeling her tight and hot around him, taking him deeper and deeper, until it no longer was body to body but was soul to soul and they were soaring together, burning together, opening each other to the limits of sensation.

His troubled disposition had nothing to do with that.

It had to do with the cash.

Cash wasn't the way a man did legitimate business, not even if he was Olivier DuChesne, wealthy and powerful enough to do business in any manner he wished. Cash was for illicit transactions. It was for untraceable deals. It was the way people said, "Get lost." It was the way they bought a person's acquiescence, a person's silence.

Damn it, the whole thing just didn't feel right.

Chapter Eleven

The dining room was enormous. Its walls and absurdly high ceiling were paneled in lustrous mahogany. The floor was covered with a thick Persian rug. The table looked like something out of a medieval costume drama; it ran more than twenty feet from end to end, and the chairs lined up on either side were ornately carved, with tapestry cushions.

Only one place was set, at the table's midway point. Lowery pulled out the chair in front of the place setting and gestured for Hollis to sit.

With an uneasiness bordering on trepidation, she lowered herself into the chair. Her shower hadn't rejuvenated her; the summery floral-print dress she'd donned for dinner didn't make her feel the least bit festive. She gazed toward one end of the table and then the other, as if she could create another place setting by sheer will.

"Won't my father be having dinner?" she asked the butler, although she already knew the answer.

"I'm afraid he isn't feeling up to it," he said, shaking out her heavy linen napkin and draping it across her lap. "He asked me to convey his wishes for a pleasant evening. I shall bring the soup."

With that, he was gone.

Hollis rested her head in her hands and smothered a sob. It wasn't the first sob she'd had to suppress since arriving at Serault Manor. And the way things were going, she suspected it wouldn't be the last.

She could have endured all of it—the ridiculously formal dinner, the news that her father's family was in Europe, the frustration that her father wasn't feeling well enough to meet her, the hauteur of the butler and the oppressively gray demeanor of the maid—if only Ray were with her. The visit to Serault Manor was definitely peculiar, but she had survived difficult situations in her past, and she was certain she could survive this one, too.

What left her less certain was whether she could survive Ray's betrayal. When she closed her eyes, she visualized not the gaudy ceiling of the foyer, not the elaborate furnishings of her room, not the news that she apparently wasn't going to meet her long-lost family. So many disappointments, but all she could picture was Ray taking that fat envelope of cash, tucking it into his pocket and leaving.

Her head hurt. Her stomach churned. She was fatigued and distressed, and none of that mattered as much as the fact that her heart was broken.

She loved Ray. And he had sold her to that cadaverous-looking butler for an envelope stuffed with money.

Lowery reentered the room, wheeling a serving cart. It took him some time to cover the distance from the door to her chair. She stared at him, listened to the faint squeak of the wheels and stubbornly refused to thank him as he filled a glass with white wine and set a bowl of cold cucumber soup down in front of her.

From a great distance she heard a chime. Lowery continued arranging things around the gilded china plate before her: a crystal salt cellar, a pepper mill, a matching gilded bread plate containing a floury biscuit and a pat of butter molded into a rose.

She heard the chime again. "Is that the doorbell?" she asked. *Doorbell* seemed too mundane a term for the deep, resonant sound.

Lowery offered a brief, almost imperceptible nod. Then he swept out of the room.

Hollis tasted the soup and winced. It was strangely spiced, much too peppery. She sipped a little wine, which was so dry it made her mouth pucker. Setting down her glass, she concentrated on the front door.

Maybe Ray was the person who'd rung the bell. Maybe he had come to his senses, and he was right this minute standing on the porch with his envelope of cash, prepared to buy Hollis back.

Not that she would thank him for it. Oh, she'd leave Serault Manor, all right—without a backward glance. But once she was out of this spooky mansion she would tell Ray where he could stuff his empty envelope. And then she would return to Vanderville, to her quiet, solitary life, and try to forget any of this had ever happened.

Please, she prayed, folding her hands and bowing her head, *please let it be Ray at the door.*

Too restless to sit, she pushed away from the table. When she stood, a tide of exhaustion surged over her, and she nearly sank into her seat. Gripping the back of her chair, she waited until she had regained her balance. Then she tiptoed to the door at the far end of the room.

Lowery's voice was muffled by the curved hallways and distorted by the outlandish dimensions of the foyer, but she was able to make out his words. "I'm sorry, Mr. Marais, but he isn't receiving visitors this evening."

"Well, y'all might at least tell him his uncle Henri is here" came an unfamiliar voice, thick with New Orleans inflection.

"I'm sorry, Mr. Marais. He is resting. He will see no one tonight."

"Has the doctor been in today?"

"He looked in on Mr. DuChesne this morning."

"My nephew hasn't been drinking, has he?"

"Mr. DuChesne has been following the doctor's orders."

The stranger said nothing for a moment. "Well, I wish he hadn't sent the others off on that cruise. Seems the end is closing in on him dreadfully fast."

"He continues to hold his own, Mr. Marais."

"Nevertheless . . ." A pause, and then the stranger said, "Perhaps I'll drop by tomorrow."

"Very well, Mr. Marais. I shall tell him you were here."

Hollis heard a thud as the front door was closed. She scampered back to her chair, even though she was under no obligation to remain seated throughout the meal. And what law said she wasn't allowed to eavesdrop?

Her head still throbbed, but she shunted the pain aside and focused her brain power on the brief conversation she'd overheard. Her first thought was that if the man was Olivier DuChesne's uncle, then he was her great-uncle. He was her family. Why hadn't she been allowed to meet him?

For the same reason she wasn't being allowed to meet her stepmother and the twins. They hadn't coincidentally taken a vacation; they had been shipped off.

Did her father want to spare them the horror of watching him die? No, it couldn't be that. He'd been dying for some time. It seemed odd that he would choose to spare them at this late date.

Which left only one other explanation: he'd sent them away deliberately to keep them from Hollis. Maybe he hadn't told them about her, and he was doing whatever he could to make sure they never learned of her existence. He had brought her to New Orleans so he could buy her eternal silence before he himself was eternally silenced.

It seemed like the sort of ploy Olivier DuChesne would try. Years of habit compelled her to assume the worst of him.

But she resisted that obvious assumption, and tried to give him the benefit of the doubt. His decision to contact Hollis could be viewed as a noble act. Perhaps his intentions had been equally noble regarding his wife and the twins. Maybe he had wanted to meet Hollis alone, granting the two of them an opportunity to bond before the rest of the DuChesne clan was dragged into the picture. Maybe he'd sent his wife and children away out of respect for Hollis.

Believing him capable of doing something decent was a stretch. She sipped her wine, tried to ignore the thrumming pain in her head and forced down another spoonful of soup.

Lowery returned to the dining room to clear away her soup bowl. He clicked his tongue at how little she'd eaten. "It's too spicy," she said.

"New Orleans cuisine tends toward the piquant," he told her. "I hope you like the prawns."

She didn't. The main course was better than the soup, but the shellfish left an aftertaste that made Hollis wonder whether they'd turned. No, Lowery assured her when she mentioned it to him. He and Minnie had eaten some, and they'd tasted just fine. Hollis would simply have to get used to Creole cooking.

"I'm really not hungry," she said when Lowery queried her about dessert. "It's been a long day."

"Very well, then. If you'd like, I'll have some coffee sent up to your room."

Hollis told him she'd like that very much. She wanted to escape from the vast, echoing dining room.

She had barely entered her bedroom when Minnie knocked on her door. Hollis let her in, then stepped out of the way as the maid carried to the desk a tray filled with coffee fixings. After pouring a cup for Hollis, she took her leave.

Hollis closed the door and shrugged off her growing edginess. Minnie had the most bloodless complexion she had ever seen. And Lowery had all the warmth of a lizard. Being alone, even though she felt terribly isolated, was better than remaining in their company.

She crossed to the desk and took a sip of coffee. The harsh, burnt flavor made her cringe. She recalled Ray's complaints about how watery the coffee up in

Vanderville was. He had boasted that Louisiana coffee put hair on one's chest.

After taking another sip of the potent brew, Hollis could believe it.

Sighing, she crossed to the French doors and opened them. Evening had drained the air of its oppressive mugginess, and a mild breeze rippled over her face as she stepped out onto the balcony and leaned against the railing. Below her lay the stone patio, the sculpted shrubs, a narrow swath of grass and then a seven-foot-high stone wall topped with wrought iron. The word *fortress* lodged in her mind.

If she had long hair, she would let it down over the side of the railing like Rapunzel. Maybe a Prince Charming could climb up and into her private chamber to rescue her.

Unfortunately, in her fairy-tale fantasy, the Prince Charming had Ray Fargo's face. And she knew Ray was no prince.

Swearing quietly, she stepped back inside. She was not going to become depressed—and she was not going to sit around waiting for someone to rescue her. She didn't need to be rescued. She was going to spend a few days in the most magnificent house she'd ever seen, and she was going to meet her father as soon as he was feeling up to it. And then she was going to go home.

She didn't need a prince, charming or otherwise.

IN THE TWO HOURS HE SAT at his desk, he read a few letters, returned a few phone calls, initialed a few invoices and accepted two new cases. One involved a wealthy divorcée considering remarriage and wanting a credit check run on her fiancé. The other involved a man who believed his ex-wife was squandering his child-support payments on her new boyfriend.

Ah, love was grand. Luckily for Ray, he wasn't in love.

Just worried. Worried about the way Hollis had been practically torn from him. Worried about the way he'd been paid—or paid off—in cash. Worried about the way he'd been summarily dismissed.

Evaline tapped on his door and then peeked in. "It's six o'clock, boss," she said. "I'm heading for home."

"Sure. I'll lock up."

"Don't bother trying to get through all that," she said, waving toward the pile of papers that had accumulated during his absence. "Tomorrow's another day."

"Is that a fact?" He attempted a smile for her, but the instant she closed his door he let it drop.

No way in hell was he going to get through the pile of papers. Not with his mind wrapped around Hollis, and that damned butler, and her damned father in that damned house.

He pretended to work awhile longer, then gave up the charade, tossed his jacket over his shoulder and stalked out of the office. He had an apartment up near City Park, and his intention was to drive there, pop open a beer, read his mail and vegetate in front of the television. He had no reason to cruise through the Garden District.

Yet, once in his car, he found himself taking a turn and following a streetcar into the neighborhood of luxuriously landscaped estates.

Several blocks in, he pulled off the road, shifted into neutral and analyzed the situation. If he drove up to DuChesne's high-security gate, he doubted he would be granted entry. He'd gotten his money; he was supposed to disappear. DuChesne and his supercilious butler clearly wanted nothing more to do with him.

He drove past the gated driveway, around the corner and down to where the estate grounds widened to the edge of the sidewalk. The property was surrounded on all sides by a high stone wall. Ray parked, got out of his car and examined the wall, looking for chinks.

It didn't take long to find a niche in the stone surface. He wedged his toe in and boosted himself up, grabbing hold of the iron bars atop the stone. Then he chinned up until he could peer over the wall.

He immediately spotted Hollis standing on a tiny second-floor balcony, gazing down at the gardens below. She wore a flowery dress with a full skirt. Her hair framed her face in sable, and the evening shadows obscured her eyes. But Ray could imagine what he couldn't see, and what he imagined was beautiful—and miserable.

His arms began to ache, and he leapt down to the sidewalk. Dusting off his hands, he strode back to his car, where he settled behind the wheel and considered his options.

When he had left her that afternoon, she'd seemed to detest him. If she truly did, he wanted to hear it from her. He didn't want that stuffed-shirt butler telling him to scram; only Hollis had the right to send him on his way.

He reached for his car phone, pulled from his wallet the paper bearing DuChesne's phone number and punched in the numbers.

"DuChesne residence," the butler said.

"This is Ray Fargo. I'd like to speak to Hollis Griffin, please."

"That won't be possible," the butler said a bit too quickly.

"Why not?"

"I'm afraid she's exhausted. She's retired for the night."

Like hell. He'd just seen her standing on the balcony. "Why don't you just knock on her door and see if she'd be willing to take my call?" he suggested.

"That won't be possible. She's sleeping," the butler said. "Goodbye, Mr. Fargo."

Before Ray could argue, the line went dead.

Hollis wasn't sleeping. The butler was lying. For whatever reason, Ray was being denied access to her.

Probably her choice, he thought dolefully. She probably thought he was a reprobate for having accepted DuChesne's cash payment, and she'd ordered the butler to screen her calls so she wouldn't have to talk to him.

Once again he reminded himself she was better off without him. Safer, at least. Loving Ray was a direct route to disaster. He ought to do her a favor and leave her alone.

Yet he couldn't convince himself that she was safe in that house, on the terrace outside that high window, all alone. His intuition told him she was in trouble.

The heck with intuition. He was a professional; he didn't work by ESP. He assessed the facts. The facts in this case were that he'd brought Hollis to her father, she was currently nice and cozy in the old man's palatial house, the old man was on death's doorstep and Hollis was undoubtedly going to inherit some pretty pocket change in the not-too-distant future.

The last thing she needed in her life was a meddling detective like Ray.

HOLLIS TOOK another shower before bed. She wasn't sure why, except that she was bored and itchy and out of sorts. She washed her hair, dried it with one of the plush white towels Minnie had left for her and slipped into her nightgown. She got into the bed, thumbed listlessly through a magazine she'd found on the night table and then slammed the magazine shut and turned off the lamp.

Her head still hurt. Her stomach still felt weird. The soft cotton of her nightgown chafed her skin. Her eyes burned. She wasn't a seasoned flyer; no doubt the airplane trip, combined with the bizarre afternoon she'd spent in her father's house, had wreaked havoc with her system.

That and the ocean of tears she'd been suppressing ever since Lowery had handed Ray that envelope.

The bed was much too wide. She hadn't slept alone since the night of her gallery exhibit opening. That seemed so long ago...and yet Ray seemed so near, so very much a part of her.

He would never share her bed again, she promised herself. How could he have left her here at Serault Manor, bewildered and defenseless? She was no closer to having a father now than she'd been before Ray had barged uninvited into her life. She was more than a thousand miles from home, she felt as if someone were drilling holes through her brain, and Ray, the first man she'd ever loved, had turned out to be a rat.

For money. He'd seduced her for the money, and he'd abandoned her for the money.

She rolled over, punched her pillow and hugged her stomach. She would feel better tomorrow. So, she hoped, would her father. They'd have their reunion, and everything would be all right.

She slept fitfully, besieged by strange, frightening dreams. Dreams of her father's death, her mother's, dreams of joining them in some eternal, bottomless world of darkness. She dreamed of Ray holding her, fusing his mouth to hers, fusing his body to hers, stealing her heart and walking away. She dreamed of bitter black coffee, as thick as tar.

She awakened feeling nauseated. Minnie was standing over her with a breakfast tray.

"I'm not hungry," Hollis said, shocked to hear how scratchy her voice sounded.

"You've got to eat something," Minnie said, setting the tray down on the bed beside Hollis. "My mama always said breakfast is the most important meal of the day."

Hollis eyed the plate of fresh fruit, the croissants, the butter and the coffeepot. It did look delicious, and she'd eaten little of her dinner last night. Maybe what she was feeling wasn't nausea but hunger.

"Okay," she said, pouring herself a cup of the viscous black brew. "Thank you, Minnie. I'm sure I'll enjoy this."

Minnie hovered over her for a minute, as if she didn't quite believe Hollis was going to eat it. She took a long sip of the wretched coffee, then tore a chunk from one of the croissants and stuffed it into her mouth. Chewing, she glared defiantly at Minnie, who retreated to the door and left the room.

Alone, Hollis nearly spit out the croissant. Like everything else she'd eaten since arriving at Serault Manor, the flaky biscuit had an odd aftertaste. She drank a little more coffee, then tried another bite of the roll. And a little more coffee.

The upheaval in her stomach was so sudden, so painful, she almost didn't make it to the bathroom in time. She kneeled in front of the toilet as wave after wave of nausea rolled over her. When at last she was empty, she felt too weak to stand.

"I'm sick," she muttered.

Her conclusion was so obvious she smiled, but her smile vanished when a fresh surge of nausea seized her. She bowed over the bowl, heaving, racked with pain.

The flu, she decided. Either that, or a reaction to the local water, some domestic form of turista. No wonder she'd felt so odd all day yesterday; she was incubating a ghastly little disease.

She pulled herself from the floor until she was leaning against the pedestal sink. Her hands shook as she twisted the faucets, as she doused her face and rinsed her mouth. When she straightened and reached for her towel, the room whirled around her. She grabbed the sink and groaned.

Somehow, she staggered back to bed. No more food, she promised herself. Just liquids until she was feeling better.

Minnie arrived to pick up the tray. "Y'all hardly touched your breakfast," she scolded.

"I'm sick. Could you bring me some tea?"

"Tea and juice," Minnie decided. Hollis managed a weak nod.

A few minutes later, Lowery appeared, carrying a pot of tea. "Minnie tells me you aren't feeling well," he said, his face revealing no emotion. He was obviously used to being around sick people.

"I'm going to rest," she said, then thanked him when he handed her a cup of tea. Like everything else, it tasted funny—but now she knew why: her taste buds were apparently affected by her illness. "I'd like a basin," she added, thinking about how violently ill she'd been just a few minutes ago.

"I'll see to it. You finish this tea."

She did, although it was a struggle. When the cup was empty, she collapsed against the pillows, shivering. Her skin was clammy with perspiration. Her legs felt weak. She closed her eyes.

The room began to rotate wildly. Opening her eyes, she gripped the mattress and gasped for breath. The bed seemed to tremble under her; the ceiling spun. She leaned over the edge of the mattress, thankfully finding a basin on the night table.

She stumbled on her way to the bathroom, but broke the fall by grabbing the desk. She could think of nothing she'd ever done that was as arduous as walking the rest of the way to the bathroom.

Resuming her position in front of the toilet, her knees bruised by the cold marble tiles of the floor, she moaned. She'd had the flu before, but never like this. In fact, she'd always responded with disbelief when she'd read about people dying of it. Now she believed the bug could be fatal.

I'm not going to die, she told herself, even as her vision blurred and her hands clung desperately to the commode. *I'm very sick, but I'm not going to die. I'll see a doctor and get well.*

With painstaking caution, she stood. Her legs felt like fragile glass under her, too weak to bear her weight. She groped along the walls, pausing twice to catch her breath on her way back to her bed. She had just fallen across the blanket when Lowery walked in with a fresh pot of tea.

"I need Ray," she whispered.

"You need a cup of tea," he countered, pouring one for her.

She struggled to sit up so she could sip the tea without spilling it. Had she just said she needed Ray? She must be delirious. What she needed was a doctor, someone who could cure her. Not a duplicitous bastard like Fargo, not a man who could make the most heavenly love to a woman and think of it as nothing more than a job, one for which he expected to be paid generously.

"I need Ray," she whispered again, as if her mouth had become disconnected from her brain.

"That will not be possible," Lowery said. "He's on to other jobs, and you're here."

"I need . . ." Her voice emerged faint and breathless and her throat was raw. She sipped a little tea to soothe it, then shook her head. "You don't understand. I need a doctor. I need Ray."

"Have some more tea," Lowery urged her. "The more tea you drink, the sooner you'll be over this malaise."

"I want to see a doctor."

"Doctors don't make house calls."

"Yes, they do. The doctor comes to see Olivier DuChesne. I want the doctor to see me, too."

"No doctor comes to see your father."

She began to cry. Not for Ray, not for her being stranded in a strange house, unable to see the man she'd traveled all this way to meet, but simply because she felt so dreadful. Why did she keep saying things that made no sense? Why was she so positive that these nonsensical statements *did* make sense?

Why, after he'd used her, exploited her and abandoned her, did she still want Ray, want him so badly, her body seemed to burn with need?

Not need. Fever. She was sick. She didn't need Ray.

"I need Ray," she mouthed, too weak to vocalize the words. Lowery took the cup from her a second before she fell against the cool, fluffy pillow and let sleep wash over her.

She heard voices... Her mother saying, *I named you Annabelle for his mother. I begged him to acknowledge you. She's your child, I said. She's ours.*

Sheila saying, *You look like hell.*

Ray saying, *I'll doom you.*

She heard other voices. Lowery and another man, not the man from last night but someone else. Maybe her father, out in the hall.

She wasn't sure whether she was asleep or awake, and she didn't care. In a trance, she hauled herself out of bed, staggered to the door, yanked it open and fell to her knees in the hall. It was empty, but she still heard voices.

She crawled along the runner rug. The roses and vines looked alive to her. She could almost feel the thorns pricking her skin, and the vines tangling around her ankles, snagging her.

She kept crawling.

"He's stable." The voice came from one of the angels in the domed ceiling above the front door.

No. She might be crazy, but she wasn't *that* crazy. The voice was coming from the foyer below and echoing off the ceiling.

"I've upped his dosage some. He should be feeling better in the morning."

"Thank you, Doctor." Lowery's voice came out of an adorable little angel's mouth. "It was good of you to stop by."

"No problem. I'll come by and see how he's doing tomorrow."

A doctor. There was a doctor here. Hollis screamed for him to come upstairs and make her better. She pumped her lungs, opened her mouth, hollered her heart out.

No sound emerged.

She began to sob, silently, curled up on the carpeted hallway. Bony hands lifted her, bony arms cradled her. She gazed up into Lowery's bony face.

"I'm dying."

"Oh, dear. What a thing to say."

"It's Ray. He killed his wife, and now he's doomed me."

"My, my. You don't know what you're saying." Lowery placed her gently on her bed and pulled the covers over her. "Try to rest, Miss Griffin. I'll bring you some more tea."

"I heard a doctor."

"No, miss, you didn't. I'm afraid the illness has deranged your mind. There was no doctor here."

"I heard you talking to him. You and the doctor and the angels in the ceiling..." Oh, God she *was* deranged.

"Get some rest. I'll prepare the tea."

She heard Lowery's footsteps growing fainter as he crossed the room, and then the click of her door being shut.

I'm doomed, she thought. *Ray brought me here and I'm going to die.*

Then sleep draped its thick black veil over her once more.

"WHAT DO YOU MEAN, she's sick?" Ray shouted into the phone.

"Miss Griffin is suffering from the flu."

"I want to talk to her!"

"I'm sorry, Mr. Fargo. That won't be possible."

If that blasted butler said, "That won't be possible," one more time, Ray would be tempted to tie the man's vocal cords in knots.

Since when couldn't a person with the flu pick up the phone and croak, "Hi, I've got the flu"? And since when could someone who had been incredibly full of life all of twenty-four hours ago become totally incapacitated by the flu in such a short time? Ray had been with Hollis every day until he'd left her at Serault Manor yesterday afternoon. She'd revealed no early symptoms, no aches or cramps or fatigue. She'd been just fine.

"She doesn't have the flu," he argued. "You don't just get the flu overnight."

"In this case, apparently, that is precisely how she has gotten it."

"Well, I still want to talk to her."

"That won't be—"

"Possible," Ray completed the sentence. A low growl caught in his throat. "When she's feeling better, have her call me."

"I believe she would rather not speak to you."

"Of course she'd rather not. She's got that kind of flu where you can't talk on the phone."

The butler didn't acknowledge Ray's sarcasm. "Before she fell ill, she said she wished to have nothing to do with you."

"Yeah, well, I want to hear her say that to me herself."

"I'm afraid that won't be poss—"

Ray slammed down the phone. How could Hollis be sick? He'd seen her yesterday evening, standing on the balcony. And yesterday morning—had it been that recently?—he'd seen her in her bedroom, in her bed. He had awakened with her in his arms. Even before she'd been fully conscious, he had moved his leg between her thighs and flexed it, and she'd purred and arched toward him, and stayed with him as he'd rolled onto his back. She'd kissed him, strummed her hands up and down his body and ridden him until they were both gasping, laughing, trembling with ecstasy.

He had never felt more alive in his life. Neither, he suspected, had she. A person couldn't be that intensely alive one day, and too ill to use the telephone the next.

Why the hell wouldn't she talk to him—even if only to tell him to get lost? Hollis wasn't the sort of woman who made other people do her dirty work. She'd been speaking for herself all her life, as far as Ray could tell. There was no reason on earth she would suddenly lack the guts to tell Ray where to get off.

Unless... unless what she had was worse than the flu. Unless she was *really* sick.

Or unless that gasbag butler was forbidding her to talk to Ray, keeping her locked away for some unfathomable purpose.

He had to see her. If only to prove to himself that he hadn't led her into danger the way he'd led another woman into danger so many years ago, a woman whose death he would never forgive himself for causing....

He had to see Hollis.

UNDER HER NOSE was a cup of tea. Bleary, too weak to sit, Hollis stared at the gaunt butler, at the delicate china cup he was holding against her lips, at the murky brown fluid sending steam into her face.

"I'll drink it," she promised. "In a minute." Her mouth hurt. Her gums ached. Her tongue and her inner cheeks tingled. Merely smelling the tea made her gag.

"Drink it now. It will make you feel better."

"In a while." She lay back against the pillows and closed her eyes.

She was still half-asleep. Her lungs burned with every breath. Her eyes felt gritty. An incessant hum buzzed through her skull.

She was sicker than ever. Yet somehow, as her body slipped further and further away from her control, her mind grew sharper and sharper. And it told her that she wasn't just dying.

She was being poisoned.

She didn't know why, but she knew it. The tea, the coffee, the soup, the breakfast croissant—everything she'd eaten since she'd arrived at Serault Manor had tasted funny.

Someone was trying to kill her.

Ray wasn't going to save her. No one else beyond the walls of the estate was aware that she was here. She would die and no one would ever know.

She'd be damned if she wouldn't put up a fight.

She lay immobile, her wheezing breath regular and her eyes closed. If Lowery thought she was asleep, he would stop trying to get her to drink the tea.

She listened. After a long while, she heard him leave the room. The door clicked loudly as he shut it.

She opened her eyes, rolled onto her side and exerted herself to swing her legs around and place her feet on the floor. She had hardly any feeling in her soles; she wondered if her toes had already died.

Ray, she thought, hurling herself onto the floor. *Ray, I will never forgive you for abandoning me. I will never, ever forgive you for letting them kill me.*

Inch by agonizing inch, she crawled across the room to the French doors. She lacked the strength to open them—and then a burst of energy infused her and she raised herself high enough to grab the brass door handle. The door eased open.

She crawled out onto the balcony. The air smelled of late-blooming rhododendrons, of grass and humidity. It smelled of life.

Ray, she thought, fighting through her weariness, pulling herself hand over hand, until she could prop herself up on the railing. *I will never stop hating you for this....*

Two stories below her extended the stone patio. If she jumped, the fall would probably kill her.

If she stayed, the tea would definitely kill her.

She leaned against the railing, ordered her fingers to hike up her nightgown and used her hands to lift one numb leg over the top, and then the other.

Damn you, Ray Fargo, she cried—and jumped.

Chapter Twelve

Ray didn't care for disguises, but he accepted their necessity when the occasion called for them. Like now.

Before driving to the Garden District, he had decked himself out in a fake mustache, a cap and dark sunglasses. He'd stuffed a wad of chewing gum into his mouth, swapped cars with Evaline and affixed a commercial logo on the door of her car. At the gate to Serault Manor, he stared into the camera and said, in an artificially nasal voice, "I got a delivery here for a Mr. Oliver Du-chez-nee."

"Du-*shane.*" The butler corrected him through the speaker.

"Yeah, whatever. It's gotta be signed for."

"Very well."

Ray heard the familiar static, and then the gate swung open.

He stopped his car halfway through the gate so it couldn't be closed. He might have fooled the butler on the video camera, but face-to-face, Ray knew the old toad would have little trouble identifying him—or, at least, his voice. Especially since he'd already made a general nuisance of himself with his attempts to reach Hollis.

His plan was to avoid the front door and head straight for the second-story balcony where he'd seen her standing the previous evening. Hanging from his belt was a rope with a grappling hook tied to one end, in case he had to scale the wall. He hoped it wouldn't come to that, though. He would be satisfied just to see her safe and healthy—or even safe and suffering from the flu. In any case, safe enough to look him in the eye and tell him in her own voice to go to hell.

If he heard the words from Hollis herself, he would accept them. Once he knew his relationship with her hadn't placed her in jeopardy, he could get on with his life.

He hurtled over a hedge and raced across the lawn, moving toward the side of the house at a speed most track stars would envy. Around the house he flew, his legs straining, his hands pumping. And then he saw her, balanced precariously on the wrought-iron railing, about to hurl herself onto the flagstones below.

She was neither safe nor healthy. Her hair was matted, her complexion the color of cold ashes, her eyes unfocused, her lips dry and cracked. She teetered, her hands unable to hold herself steady as she straddled the railing and stared down at the patio.

Ray whispered a prayer, then broke through the sculpted shrubs. He didn't know whether she saw him—or, if she did, whether she knew who he was. Even without the sunglasses and fake mustache, he doubted she would know who he was. She seemed completely out of it.

More than out of it. Suicidal. What the hell had happened to the Hollis Griffin he knew, that strong, beautiful, talented woman on the cusp of fame? What had DuChesne done to her?

She brought her other leg over the railing, and Ray prayed he would have a chance to ask her. He closed the distance until he was almost directly underneath her, planted his feet and extended his arms.

The impact of her plunging weight pitched him backward, but he managed to cushion her fall with his body. Through the thin cotton of her nightgown he felt the gangly tangle of her limbs. Her head bumped against his shoulder and she moaned.

He moaned, too. He'd had the wind knocked out of him, and his back had slammed into the unyielding stones of the patio. But even after taking the brunt of her fall, he knew he was in much better condition than she was.

She sucked in a shallow, wheezy breath. As he pushed himself up to sit, she shifted against him, a slack heap of bones held together by papery skin. "Breathe," he demanded, giving her a shake.

Another wheezy breath. He cupped her head in his hands and turned her to face him. Her eyes fluttered open, but they were flat, dull, unseeing.

He cursed. She looked feverish but she felt cold. She was so pale, so inert.

He heard someone shouting in the distance. There was no time to slap her cheeks and rouse her, no time to question her on what was wrong and where she was hurt. He hoisted her over his shoulder, feeling her arms and head dangle lifelessly against his back, and ran around the mansion to his car. The gate pinched the car's doors, as if someone had tried to close it.

"I'm not going to let you die," he vowed, sprinting the last few yards, yanking the gate out of his way and dropping her onto the front seat. He shoved her toward the passenger side, jumped in next to her, revved the engine and slammed the car into reverse, his gaze fixed on his rearview mirror.

Once they were several blocks away from Serault Manor and he caught his breath, he tore off the mustache and turned to view her. She was slumped down in the seat, her head resting against the door and her legs jammed under the glove compartment.

Refusing to acknowledge his dread, he rearranged her so she was sitting higher and strapped her seat belt around her. She was still breathing—that horrid whistling breath, but it was better than no breath at all. Her lips moved as he stroked her cheeks, and she moaned.

"I'm going to get you help, Hollis," he murmured. "You're going to be all right, *chère.* You're going to be fine."

He slid back behind the wheel and pulled into the traffic, heading for the nearest hospital.

He parked at the emergency entrance, shot around to the passenger door and gathered her limp body into his arms. "You just hang on, darlin'," he murmured as he carried her up the ramp to the double doors. "They're going to make you well, Hollis. They're going to make everything better." She probably couldn't hear him, but he spoke the words anyway, desperate to reassure himself.

Inside, he strode past the assorted people in the waiting area and presented himself to the harried-looking nurse at the reception desk. "This woman is dying," he said. "She needs immediate attention."

"What's wrong with her?"

"I don't know. That's for a doctor to figure out."

"What's her name?"

"Hollis Griffin."

"Does she have insurance?"

"Damn it, just get a doctor here to look at her. I'll pay whatever it costs."

Unsure of what to do, the nurse beckoned Ray behind a curtained area, where an empty bed stood. He put Hollis down, and she moaned again. The nurse scurried off.

He centered her head on the small foam pillow and brushed her hair back from her clammy cheeks and forehead. "Listen to me, Hollis," he said, his lips close to her ear. "Nothing's supposed to happen to you, okay? I don't love you. You're safe, Hollis, because—I swear to God—I don't love you."

The nurse returned, accompanied by a man in a white coat, with a name tag identifying him as Dr. Reginald Cooper fastened above the pocket. "Y'all go wait outside, now," he ordered Ray, who reluctantly complied.

Feeling utterly helpless, Ray paced the small waiting area. He tuned out the whining children, the man babbling to himself in a corner of the room, the chirping pagers and pealing telephones. His mind could absorb nothing except the woman on the other side of the curtain, the woman lying, dying, on that hospital bed.

It was his fault. Whatever happened to Hollis, whatever *had* happened to her or *would* happen to her.... Just like his wife, so long ago, Hollis was sliding toward death because of Ray, because he'd brought her into danger's path.

Because he'd let himself care about her.

You don't love her, he reminded himself. *Just because you had an affair with her, just because something incredible happened between you and her up in New York... It isn't love, so she's got to be all right.*

More phones rang. Low voices droned, loud voices shouted, wheeled carts full of glassware rattled past. A nurse approached Ray as he was completing his third lap up and down a short hallway off the waiting room.

"Excuse me," she said.

Ray halted and studied her face, trying to read Hollis's prognosis in the nurse's kind brown eyes.

"Y'all can go now," she said. "We've received a call from Olivier DuChesne. His wife is a major benefactor of our hospital, you know. He said he was glad to hear we're treating Miss Griffin, and he'll be paying all her bills. He's sending a representative over here right now to take care of the paperwork. He said to thank y'all for bringing Miss Griffin in, and you can go on home now."

Ray wanted to scream, punch a wall and then call the police. But he wisely restrained himself. He had to get Hollis out of the hospital before DuChesne's "representative"—that murderous butler, or whoever had brought Hollis to this dire condition—showed up.

"Let me just say goodbye to her, and then I'll leave," he requested. At the nurse's nod, he hurried back down the hall to the curtained area, passing Dr. Cooper, who was conferring with another nurse, and pushed back the curtain.

Hollis was still lying on the bed, unmoving. Her eyes were open, but they remained flat and spiritless, staring blindly at the ceiling.

Ray bowed over her, breaking into her line of vision. "Hollis," he whispered. "What did they do to you?"

"Ray?" She barely had the breath to carry the single word.

"I won't let them hurt you," he swore. "I won't let them get you back. What happened to you?"

"You bastard," she mouthed, then closed her eyes.

Well, he thought wryly. Maybe she was on the road to recovery, after all.

A nurse entered the partitioned area, rolling in a hooked metal frame and toting a bottle of intravenous fluid. "You'll have to leave now," she informed him. "I've got to get an IV into the patient."

"Oh. Of course." Ray straightened up and stepped back from the bed. Assessing the nurse's position with a swift glance, he took another, slightly angled step back, and another—and tripped over the metal frame, knocking the bottle out of her hand. It hit the ground and broke, flooding the floor.

The nurse shrieked. "Oh, no! Why didn't you watch where you were going? What a mess!"

"Sorry," he lied.

Grumbling under her breath, she raced out of the curtained area. "I need a fresh IV," Ray heard her announce as the curtain dropped back into place. "And we need an orderly to mop up the mess in there...."

He hastened back to Hollis's side, avoiding the puddles as best he could. "Hang on, darlin'," he whispered, then scooped her once more into his arms and darted past the curtain.

"Say, where do you think you're going?" someone shouted at him.

He didn't stop to answer. After his breakneck run at Serault Manor with Hollis in his arms, carrying her to his car just outside the door was a snap. Once again, he tossed her onto the seat, jumped in behind the wheel and floored the gas, ignoring the irate orderly who chased him out into the lot.

"Can you buckle your seat belt?" he asked, not wanting to stop this time. For all he knew, the hospital might call the police. And while he didn't have any hesitation about discussing Hollis's situation—whatever it might be—with his erstwhile brothers in blue, he didn't want to do it with her in the car. She still hated him passionately. And she was still in too much danger from DuChesne.

Ray considered driving to another hospital with her, then thought better of it. DuChesne's wife was a benefactor at just about every hospital in the city—and for all Ray knew, DuChesne had telephoned every hospital in the city in search of Hollis. Having found her once, he could easily find her again.

Ray knew of one place where DuChesne wouldn't find her. At a red light, he reached across the seat and stretched the seat belt around her inert body. The light turned green and he shot through the intersection, aiming west.

"I'm going to bring you someplace safe," he promised.

She whimpered. He cast a quick look her way. She looked even paler, if such a thing was possible. Her hands twitched in her lap, frail and so translucent he could see the blue tracings of her blood vessels. Her fingernails looked like wax, her bones sharp enough to puncture her skin.

"You're going to be all right, darlin'. Anyone who's got the good sense to call me a bastard can't be that sick."

She inhaled, then coughed feebly.

"This is one bastard who's going to keep you safe or die trying," he swore, pressing harder on the gas pedal.

The heavy, murky scent of the river entered the car through his open window. Civilization trailed behind as he navigated into an overgrown, run-down neighborhood of swamp shacks huddled in the shadow of the levee. Not too many people lived on the batture anymore, which suited Ray just fine.

He had bought his batture house on an impulse five years ago. "*House*" was as inaccurate a term for the ramshackle cabin as it was for a palace like Serault Manor. During the months it took Ray to repair the pilings, patch the roof, bring in a chemical toilet and reconstruct the porch, time and hard labor had forced him to break out of his emotional paralysis. By the time the batture house was in fit condition, so was Ray.

He could have sold the shack and made a small profit, but he didn't. It was a place where he could come when he needed to get away from life and listen to the river. If folks had to reach him, they could leave a message on the answering machine in his uptown apartment, or the one at his office. The batture house was where he went when he didn't want to be reached.

He had healed here. Maybe Hollis could heal, too.

If not, if he'd made the biggest mistake of his life by taking her away from the medical experts... Hell, he'd already made the biggest mistake of his life, and hers, when he'd gotten involved with her.

He pulled to a stop on the rutted dirt road that led to his cabin. Then he eased Hollis out of the car and into his arms. She felt ominously light to him, as if she'd lost not just a few pounds of flesh but a part of her soul.

Carrying her up the wooden steps to the porch, he murmured to her, words as soft and soothing as the constant hush of the river. Inside the three-room cabin, he brought her directly to the bed and laid her down.

She groaned, and her hands began to twitch again. Her eyelids were as blue as her fingers, he realized. The skin of her throat was so taut, he could discern the ridges in her neckbone.

"I'm going to get you some help, Hollis," he said.

Her only response was a spasmodic shiver.

He left the house and jogged down the rickety construction of planks and pilings that served as a walkway along the water's edge. He had heard that the swampy waterfront batture used to be home to hundreds of cabins, but most of them had been torn down in the fifties to make construction of the levee easier. Fewer than two dozen cabins remained, and although the neighbors kept to themselves, they also looked out for one another.

He knocked on Nanny Carre's door. Now in her eighties, Nanny had often told him about her life as a nurse, her knowledge of herbal remedies and her passing familiarity with voodoo. During the months Ray was pulling himself together, she used to brew exotic potions for him. "They'll take the edge off your grief," she'd promised. "They ain't drugs and they ain't booze. I guess you could call 'em heart medicine, on account of they'll mend your heart."

He wasn't sure how much they helped, but they certainly hadn't hurt. At the time, he'd had nothing better to believe in, so he'd believed in her mystical mumbo jumbo.

He would have to believe in it again, for Hollis's sake.

"Nanny, I need your help," he said when she appeared in the doorway. "I've got a very sick woman in my bed."

Nanny didn't laugh, didn't chastise him, didn't ask him to elaborate. She merely quirked a sparse gray eyebrow, disappeared for several moments, reappeared holding a worn cloth sack and followed him down the walkway to his cabin.

He let her go inside alone, and waited on the porch. A sleepy mist rode above the river; to the north he saw a barge, longer than a football field, gliding inland. Through the screen door he heard Nanny's voice, mumbling incomprehensibly. He didn't hear Hollis at all.

Ten minutes passed. Twenty. Ray watched the sky fade into dusk. He wondered whether he was a thousand kinds of fool for bringing Hollis here. That nurse at the hospital had been about to pump her full of the best remedies modern medicine could offer. What could Nanny Carre do compared to that?

Maybe this was the doom Ray was bringing down upon Hollis: not merely sending her to DuChesne's, but then kidnapping her from the hospital and bringing her here so an octogenarian herbalist could mutter incantations over her while she died.

By the end of an hour he could no longer sit still. "Nanny," he said, entering the house and marching into the bedroom.

The old woman shifted in her chair, where she sat beside the bed. She held a bowl in her lap, a spoon in one hand.

"How is she?" he asked.

"This young lady's been pizened," the old woman said.

"Poisoned?"

"Her innards is shot to hell," the woman continued. "Y'all know what she ate?"

He shook his head. "Whatever it is, I'm not the one who fed it to her."

"Oh, now, don't y'all go defending yerself. I know you, Ray. You're a good boy."

"What are you giving her?"

"Soup. It's got good things in it. She's not keeping much of it down. If I can't get it into her, it ain't gonna help her none."

"Can I help?"

The old woman set down the bowl, pulled a scrap of paper from a pocket in her housedress and scribbled something on it. "There's a conjure lady up on Decatur Street. You bring this to her. She'll give you some herbal powders. Don't let her charge you more'n ten dollars for them."

"I'll be back as soon as I can," he promised, grateful for something to do.

Back in the French Quarter, he stopped at the office to trade Evaline's car back for his own, and then found the address Nanny had given him, down a brick alley and up two flights of wooden stairs. A tall, thin woman with her hair wrapped in a black turban read Nanny's note and measured several powders into small plastic bags. She charged Ray twenty dollars, and he paid without a quibble. In less than an hour he was back at the cabin.

Nanny was still trying to force soup into Hollis. Hollis was still lying on the bed, ghostly pale and twitching. "How's she doing?" he asked, even though looking at her provided all the answer he could bear.

Nanny shook her head. "There's a mushroom," she said. "Death cap, it's called. It sometimes causes convulsions like this. Usually it's fatal."

"Mushrooms," Ray murmured, picturing Hollis's amazing photographs. She'd turned her cherished amanita into art. And now those plants were stealing her life from her.

"Don't know how much she's got in her system. It's a miracle she ain't dead yet."

"Make more miracles," Ray pleaded. "Keep her alive."

"I'll do my best. Meantime, could y'all fix me a sandwich? I got a long night ahead of me."

Ray prepared two cheese-and-tomato sandwiches for Nanny, then opened a bottle of beer and returned to the porch. Night was closing in. A foghorn sounded over the river, low and mournful.

Why would DuChesne have poisoned Hollis? He'd wanted to see her before he died. He'd wanted to see her so badly, he'd offered Ray a huge reward for bringing her to him.

A reward paid in cash.

If DuChesne murdered Hollis, what was the worst that could happen to him? Thanks to his liver disease, he was already on death row. And if Ray charged him with the murder, where was his proof that he'd brought Hollis to DuChesne, that she'd been there long enough to be poisoned? Cash proved nothing.

But why? Why would DuChesne want to kill his own daughter?

Because Ray had made love to her, that was why. It was his lot in life to love a woman and watch her die. He'd loved his wife, and she'd been murdered. He loved Hollis, and—

No! He nearly shouted it to the rising moon, to the sluggish green river drifting past his porch. *No, he didn't love Hollis!*

As if saying so might save her.

He couldn't save her. He'd caught her when she'd jumped from the balcony, but she was the one who had realized she was being poisoned, and who had risked the jump to save herself. And now, with Nanny's help, maybe Hollis would save herself again. All Ray could do was wait.

And admit the truth: he did love her. For transforming mushrooms and moss into visions of beauty. For looking to the future, for forgiving, for being an optimist in spite of her miserable past. For letting go of her sorrow. For fighting Ray when she had to, and loving him when she could no longer fight him.

For having the courage to climb over the balcony railing and jump.

Oh, God, he loved her. Which meant she was doomed.

Which meant he, too, was doomed.

NANNY AWAKENED HIM at sunrise the next morning. He had fallen asleep in his hammock, and as he squinted up into the wizened face of his neighbor, he realized how stiff and cramped he was. His stomach was empty; his head ached.

"You want a miracle?" she asked.

He sprang upright, setting the hammock rocking. "Is she cured?"

"She's resting," Nanny told him. "Not what y'all might think of as the pink of health. She's taken a stroll through hell, Ray. But I think she's made it out the other side."

"Thank you." Ray hugged Nanny.

"Don't thank me. It's them herbs that conjure lady up on Decatur Street sold you. Now y'all take care of your woman today. I bathed her, but she needs rest—and as much soup as you can get into her. I left a pot of it on the stove. I'm gonna go get me some sleep."

"I owe you, Nanny."

The old woman winked. "I got some loose shingles on my roof need fixing."

"I'll build you a whole new roof. Tomorrow, if you want."

Nanny shook her head and shuffled onto the dilapidated walkway. "Y'all might wait and see if she makes it, first."

Ray watched her until she vanished into her cabin. Then he entered his own.

Hollis lay on her side in the bed, staring at him. Her eyes seemed too big for her face, her cheeks too hollow. Her lips were parched and cracked. Her hands clenched restlessly against the sheet.

He lowered himself onto the chair beside the bed and took one of her hands in his, clasping it snugly to still her fidgeting. *I love this woman,* he thought. Much as he resisted it, much as it frightened him, at that moment he was certain it was the truth.

"How do you feel?" he asked.

A vague smile flitted across her lips, and her voice emerged in a croak. "Don't ask."

"Can I get you something? Some soup?"

"No," she whispered, but he was already up, crossing to the kitchen and filling a bowl. It smelled of garlic and parsley and pepper, rich and spicy.

He carried the bowl back to the bed. Despite her refusal before he'd brought it, she eagerly consumed the entire portion.

He set the empty bowl on the rough plank floor and then took Hollis's hand again. "Where am I?" she asked, gazing around at the plain white walls, the uncurtained windows, the floor that jumped an inch between the bedroom and the front room, since the bedroom had been tacked on to the cabin years after the front room had been built. Whatever Serault

Manor was, this was the opposite: cheap, plain and humble.

"My house," he told her. "My hideaway."

"I like it," she said.

Sure, she liked it. No one was trying to murder her here. "Who made you sick, Hollis?"

"I don't know. Lowery, I think."

"Lowery?"

"The butler. But..." She sighed. "He works for DuChesne. They lied to me, Ray. They lied and lied. They told me no doctor would come to the house to see me, but I heard a doctor's voice in the house. I know he was there, and they wouldn't let me see him. They wouldn't let me see anyone. I never even saw my father..." Her voice dissolved into a sob.

He shoved back the chair, kicked off his shoes and climbed onto the bed beside her. The mattress sagged slightly; the iron headboard creaked. He pulled her into his arms and held her tight.

She cried. She clung to him, huddled against him, shuddered within his embrace. Her body heaved against him. Her tears soaked his shirt.

He wanted never to let her go.

Eventually she wept herself dry. With a final shiver, she sniffled and drew back. And punched him in the stomach.

He grunted, even though the jab didn't hurt at all. "What was that for?"

"Selling me," she snapped.

"Selling you?"

"He paid you for me. In cash. I saw."

Ray frowned. "That bothered me, too."

"Not enough to turn down the money. You sold me to murderers, Ray—"

He pulled her back into his arms, not caring if she wanted to punch him again. He wove his fingers through her hair and brushed it back from her damp, flushed cheeks. Gazing into her eyes, he said, "That money's sitting untouched in a safe-deposit box. It puzzled me as much as you, Hollis. I don't know what the hell it's about."

"You expect me to believe that?" she asked, sounding just a touch uncertain. "He was paying you to find me, right from the start. Five hundred dollars a day, plus expenses."

"I get paid to work, Hollis. It's my job."

"You get paid in cash?"

"No. I don't know why he did that—except that it troubled me something fierce. That was why I kept calling Serault Manor, kept demanding to speak to you."

"You never called!"

"I called more times than I can count. They told me you didn't want to talk to me."

"They never told me."

"I knew something was wrong, Hollis. From the moment they gave me that cash I knew, and my suspicions just got worse when they wouldn't let me talk to you. So I sneaked onto the property and found you, just when you were about to jump to your death."

She frowned and shook her head. "That wasn't you, Ray. It was a man with a mustache and dark glasses...."

"It was me wearing a disguise."

She gazed at him in astonishment. "I thought—I saw that man and I had this flash that it was you. But then I knew it couldn't be you and . . . and I realized I was crazy."

"You were never further from crazy. Jumping into my arms was the sanest thing you ever did." He stroked his hands through her hair again. "Help me out, Hollis. Help me figure out why they wanted to kill you."

"I don't know." She sighed and shuddered again, and he prepared himself for a fresh spate of tears. She didn't cry, though. She simply nestled against him, her legs shifting beneath the sheet, beneath her nightgown. "So you were the one who caught me when I jumped?"

"I was."

"That means you saved my life."

"It means I kept you from breaking your neck. That's all."

"You saved my life," she insisted, propping herself up on one shaky arm and staring at him. He sensed the strain in her, the enormous effort it cost her simply to hold herself up.

He eased her onto her back and rose above her. Her eyes transfixed him, filled with love and rage, and trust. More trust than he deserved.

Sooner or later it would dawn on her that he'd risked her life more than saved it. But for that one moment, as she gazed up at him and trusted him, he wanted to take what she had to give, and give her back everything he had.

Lowering himself into her arms, he kissed her.

Chapter Thirteen

She ought to have felt exhausted. She had run a marathon through treacherous territory. She'd had nausea, chills and hallucinations. She'd choked on the concoctions that kind, elderly woman had spooned into her. She'd moaned and clawed at the bed linens and begged God for mercy, for life or death but no more limbo.

The limbo was over, and she'd surfaced on the side of life.

And there was Ray. She had suspected him of having doomed her, but he had in fact rescued her. Without him, she would be dead.

Without him, she couldn't imagine living.

She met his lips with hers, lifted her arms to circle him and pulled him down onto her. He was as solid as life itself, as strong and warm and vibrant. His mouth was gentle but insistent, coaxing, teasing, demanding. When her lips parted, he stole inside. When her tongue met his, she felt the fiery urgency of life spread through her body, melting the last, lingering chills of her bout with death, chasing away what was left of her terror.

"When I was so sick," she whispered, raking her fingers through his hair and tracing his cheeks with her thumbs, "I kept calling for you. And you came."

"I was almost too late."

"But you weren't. Oh, Ray—I didn't even know why, but I knew I had to have you."

"You have me now, *chère.*"

"You called me that before," she said, unsure of when he'd used that term, or why she remembered. Somewhere in the shadowy depths of her memory, she recalled the echo of his voice and the power of his arms around her, carrying her, cradling her. She recalled the drumming of his heartbeat as he held her high against his chest. Through the fog of her delirium, through the horror of it, she remembered.

"It means beloved," he told her, and kissed her again.

Her fingers felt stiff and clumsy to her as she slid them down to his jaw, his neck, his shoulders. It was as if she had to learn all over again how they worked, what they could do. When she reached the top button of his shirt she fumbled, unable to accomplish the simplest of tasks.

He gathered her hands in his, lifted them to his lips and kissed them, again and again—palms, knuckles, the tips of her fingers. Then he lowered her hands and kissed her lips. "Don't look so sad," he whispered. "You're going to be okay."

"I'm all thumbs. I can't even undo a button...."

"Not a problem." He easily opened his shirt and shrugged out of it. She envied him his dexterity. "It takes time to get your strength back, Hollis. Don't worry about it."

He kissed her again, and she found it impossible to worry. How could she worry when the light pressure of his mouth against the skin of her throat stirred her nerves awake, made them quiver and signal her that her strength was already returning? How could she worry when Ray was making her feel more alive than she'd ever felt before?

She lifted her hands to his shoulders, tracing their rugged contours, their hollows and ridges, before moving to his back. Having journeyed to death's door and returned, she experienced everything more keenly: the hot, sleek texture of his skin, the subtle rippling of his muscles, the weight of his hips pressing down on hers through the sheet, through his jeans and her nightgown.

He rose and stripped away the sheet. He lifted her and stripped away her nightgown. He stood and stripped off his jeans. Her vision seemed as acute as her sense of touch. When she gazed at his strong, naked body, at his streamlined physique, the healthy, potent masculinity of him, his beauty hurt her eyes.

He settled back on the bed beside her and skimmed one hand down her body to her hip. "Tell me what you can take," he murmured, then brushed his lips down past the hollow of her throat to her collarbone. "You've been through hell—"

"I'll bet I look like hell, too," she muttered.

"You look like an angel." He grazed downward to her breast. "I'm going to take you to heaven, angel," he whispered, then stroked the sensitive skin of her nipple with his tongue, scraped it with his teeth, sucked it deep into his mouth. He shifted to her other breast, kissing, nibbling, teasing it until it was hot and swollen, until her entire body felt his kiss, until her soul felt it.

He moved farther down her body, caressing her skin with his fingertips, with his lips, with his tongue. He kissed her belly, her hips, her left knee, her right ankle. Her left thigh, her right. The soft, trembling skin of her inner thighs as he moved her legs apart, as he knelt between them and bowed his head.

"Ray..." The broken, breathless sound of her voice reminded her of how she'd called out to him when she'd been dying. She felt almost as if she were dying now; the sensations he was arousing as his tongue flicked and probed and loved her were too intense. She couldn't possibly survive anything this intimate, this intense.

He had promised to take her to heaven, and as he deepened his kiss, she glimpsed it, strove toward it, felt herself rising higher and higher, closer and closer. Then suddenly her body erupted in a final surge, lofted high on the currents of passion until she no longer knew where she was, heaven or earth or some dream place in between.

All she knew, all that mattered, was that Ray had brought her there.

She grabbed his shoulders and pulled him up. His mouth opened over hers and her body opened to him. His thrusts were hard, fervent, consuming. She contracted around him, throbbed, reached for heaven again and again, luring him to the same destination, needing him there with her.

They arrived together in an instant of perfect unity. Through the golden mists of pleasure Hollis heard Ray's low, hoarse cry as he lost and then found himself inside her. It was a cry of defeat, a cry of triumph.

A cry of love.

"NO, HOLLIS," he said firmly. "I'll go alone. You'll stay here."

They were seated in his kitchen, a tiny, rustic room with a sloping floor and barely enough space for a table. She had balked when Ray offered her a cup of coffee, but when he insisted that she try it, she was pleased to discover that, while thick and strong, it didn't taste anything like that tainted brew Lowery had served her at Serault Manor. In fact, it tasted wonderful.

"That's what *real* coffee tastes like," Ray had declared.

"It's going to put hair on my chest," she complained, although she happily took another sip.

She was wearing one of his shirts. She had no clothing with her, other than her nightgown. Even if she'd had a complete wardrobe, though, she would have wanted to wrap herself up in his shirt. It was the next best thing to wrapping herself up in him.

"I have to come with you," she argued. "I'm the one they tried to kill."

"They may try to kill you again."

"Would I be any safer if I stayed here alone?"

He ruminated for a minute, then let out a weary breath. "Nobody knows you're here."

"That voodoo lady does."

"Nanny Carre isn't a voodoo lady. She's a nurse with a bit of unconventional knowledge. And after she worked so hard to cure you, she surely isn't going to reveal your whereabouts to any murderers. Now, try to remember, Hollis. What was the name you heard? The man who talked to Lowery outside the dining room."

For the past hour she had been trying to reconstruct the period she had spent at Serault Manor. Her mind was a jumble of tattered, scattered memories, distorted snapshots, close-up and fish-eye lens views, like her photos. She could see, but she didn't know what she was looking at.

She closed her eyes and concentrated. She visualized the cavernous dining room, the lone place setting, the embroidered chairs, the dark walls and the elaborate chandelier. Outside the door were voices, Lowery's and someone else's. An aged voice, an extremely Southern voice: *Tell him his uncle Henry is here.*

"Henry," she said. "Uncle Henry... something. I don't remember the last name."

"Henry DuChesne?"

She shook her head. "No. It was something else, something like..." She squeezed her eyes tighter, as if that would clarify her recollections. The butler hadn't called the man Henry, she knew that. He'd called him... "Mr. Murray?"

"Henry Murray. Great." Ray swallowed the last of his coffee and pushed back his chair. "I'll have Nanny Carre come and stay with you while I go into town and track down this Henry Murray fellow."

Hollis pushed back her own chair and stood. "I'm coming with you, Ray."

"You're too weak."

Her body might have been weak, but her resolve was strong. She was not going to sit in this cabin, breathing in the damp air of the river and waiting while Ray tracked down her would-be killers. "I'm coming with you."

"You haven't got any clothes."

"I'll borrow a pair of your pants."

He shook his head and let out a sigh. "Don't be silly. They won't fit you."

"Whether or not they fit, I'm coming with you."

He stared at her. She stared back. A long moment passed, and then he sighed and shook his head again. She had won.

She tried not to gloat—and indeed, when her vision suddenly went blurry and she had to grip the edge of the table to keep from falling, she didn't feel much like gloating. Ray reached across the table to catch her, but she warded him off with a determined look. "I'm coming with you," she declared.

Ten minutes later, wearing an old pair of Ray's jeans, with the hems cuffed several times and a rope tied around the waist because all his belts were too big, she left the cabin with him. She let him carry her—only because she had no shoes, she rationalized—and strove not to collapse in a heap when he lowered her onto the seat of the car. She felt both queasy and lightheaded, needing food but too unsettled to eat any.

That coffee hadn't been bad, though. Maybe she could have another cup once they got to his office.

She was amazed to discover how close Ray's riverside cabin was to the heart of the city. The cottages huddled along the Mississippi banks seemed so remote, so far from the noise and bustle of civilization.

Just like her house in the woods north of Vanderville, she thought, eyeing Ray with new insight. He needed a place where he could escape from the hustle and bustle, just as she did.

Why should that surprise her? She loved Ray. Of course they would both have the same needs.

Her body still shimmered with the memory of the morning's ecstasy. Simply thinking about what he'd done to her, what he'd made her feel, made her appreciate how glad she was to be alive and in love with Ray Fargo. *Chère,* he'd called her. *Beloved.* Whatever his misgivings about falling in love with her, he seemed to have overcome them.

Or had he? Why should she assume he loved her the way she loved him? Just because he'd made exquisite love to her, just because he'd caught her during her death fall from the terrace outside her window at Serault Manor, and absconded with her before her assassins could reach her at the hospital, and hidden her in his shack by the river.... Just because she owed him her very life didn't mean he loved her.

Steering the car through the clogged streets of New Orleans, he seemed withdrawn. She sensed no anger in him—for all his huffing and puffing about how she ought to stay behind while he went off in search of Henry Murray, she knew he didn't mind all that much that she'd insisted on accompanying him.

But he was withdrawing in a more fundamental way. When he looked at her, she saw not love in his eyes, as she'd seen in bed, but fear.

Maybe if she said it first, if she paved the way for him, he could acknowledge his feelings. "I love you, Ray."

He kept his eyes on the traffic. She would have concluded that he hadn't even heard her except for the ticking muscle in his jaw, the sudden tightness of his hands around the steering wheel.

He said nothing.

"Ray?"

"Don't." He set his chin, yanked the wheel and turned the corner.

"Ray—"

"I'm warning you, Hollis. You don't know what you're talking about. Let's just get this job done and leave the rest of it alone."

Fine. If he wanted to retreat behind his work, let him. He couldn't scare Hollis off that easily. She'd been to hell and back, right? She'd nearly died. What could Ray say to her that would be any worse than what she'd already lived through?

Just this: *I don't love you. I can't love you. I will never love you.*

Leave it alone, she meditated. *Get the job done.* Once she had learned the facts about her father, about the malevolent butler and that gray little maid and the evil that inhabited Serault Manor, she could focus on more important matters.

Like how she would survive losing Ray.

He parked on a narrow street lined with three-story brick buildings tiered with ornate wrought-iron balconies. "Is this the French Quarter?" she asked.

"Yes." He climbed out of the car and circled it to help her out. The sidewalk felt grimy against the soles of her feet, but if Ray didn't love her, she didn't want him carrying her. She would rather walk barefoot.

Even so, her legs were shaky. Resentfully, she let him loop his arm around her and support her as they entered one of the picturesque brick buildings and climbed the stairs to the second floor.

An attractive middle-aged woman with curly red hair and an easy smile glanced up from her computer as they entered the front room of Ray's office. Ray made the introductions. "Evaline, this is Hollis Griffin. Hollis, Evaline Hammond. Do me a favor, Evaline, and see if you can find me a Henry Murray living in the area."

Evaline's gaze wandered between Ray and Hollis. "Is this a paid job or an obsession?" she asked, her smile muting the acid in her voice.

"An obsession."

She snorted and turned back to her computer. "Just wanted to know," she drawled as she began tapping her fingers along the keyboard.

Ray ushered Hollis into an inner office. It was decorated simply—a large steel desk occupied most of the room, one wall held several file cabinets and two computers sat on a counter. A philodendron struggled toward the sunlight that spilled in through the window. Colorful print posters announcing various jazz festivals from years past adorned the walls.

Ray guided Hollis into an upholstered chair facing his desk. He moved around to the other side and settled into the swivel chair. "You want some coffee?"

She nodded.

Ray signaled his secretary through an intercom and requested two cups. Hollis watched him, measuring his gestures, his facial expressions, his overall aloofness. Perhaps he was always like this when he was immersed in a case. When she was working on her photography, a bomb could fall ten yards from her and she wouldn't notice. Some people were more focused than others.

It wasn't just focus with Ray, though. It was detachment. Denial. Retreat.

Sighing, she curled herself into the cushions of the chair, drawing her knees to her chin, smelling the clean, male scent of Ray on the apparel she wore. Evaline entered the room carrying two mugs of coffee. She set them down on the desk and said, "I can't find a Henry Murray. Have you got any other possibilities? Murrow, Morrow, Moreau—"

"It wasn't Moreau," Hollis said before Ray could speak. "But maybe it was a French name. Like DuChesne and Serault. They're all French names."

"Creole," Ray corrected her.

"Well . . . anyway, it sounded like Murray. Moray? Marie?"

Ray grabbed one of the mugs of coffee and crossed to the computer counter. He switched on a machine and began entering data.

Evaline eyed Hollis curiously. "I've got some espadrilles you can borrow. They might be a touch big, but they're better than nothing."

Hollis glanced toward Ray, who was hunched over the computer, ignoring her. She smiled gratefully at Evaline. "Thank you. And thanks for the coffee."

Evaline shot Ray a quick look, then turned back to Hollis. "Don't y'all just love those moods of his?" she muttered. Ray acted as if he hadn't heard her.

"There's a Henry Marris living in Metairie," he said.

"It wasn't Marris, I'm sure of that. It ended in a vowel sound. Marie, Maray—"

"Henri Marais," Ray announced, hitting more buttons on the computer. "An address up in Lake Vista."

Hollis sat quietly, sipping her coffee and listening as Ray dialed a phone number. "Hello. I'm looking for Mr. Henri Marais. Mr. Marais? Ray Fargo. I'm a private investigator employed by Mr. Olivier DuChesne, and I—your nephew, is he?" Hollis allowed herself a victorious smile, but Ray's face revealed nothing. "Well, yes. There's been an incident of a difficult nature, Mr. Marais, and I'd like to spare your nephew any undue publicity, given his high profile in town. If we could meet somewhere and talk discreetly..." Ray stared out the window. "Sure, I know the place. Fifteen minutes." He hung up the phone.

"I'm coming," Hollis said.

His gaze was frosty. "Suit yourself," he said. She wished he had objected—a good quarrel would prove that he at least cared what she did. But he was beyond that, too far away to fight with her.

Shuffling down the stairs in Evaline's stretched-out espadrilles, Hollis resolved not to lean on Ray, not to need him. Perhaps Henri Marais would answer her questions and explain what had happened to her at Serault Manor. Perhaps he wouldn't. Either way, she was not going to let her emotions get in her way. If Ray could be cold, so could she.

Her stoicism was tested when Ray navigated into the Garden District. The mansions looked vaguely familiar to her, the cypress and magnolia trees, the emerald lawns... When she recognized the camera-monitored gates of her father's estate, she felt her stomach heave. She had to press her fist to her mouth to stifle her anguished cry.

Ray glanced at her, and she saw a flicker of emotion in his eyes. Then he looked away, his face once again a mask of cool tension.

They arrived at a quietly elegant restaurant called the Captain's Palace. A waiter rushed over and held the car door open for her. His eyebrows lifted slightly when he saw her strange outfit, but he courteously escorted her under the awning and inside.

"Is Mr. Marais here?" Ray asked the maître d'.

"Monsieur Marais is at his usual table," the maître d' replied. "He's waiting for you."

Hollis and Ray were led into a cozy paneled room. At a secluded corner table sat a slim, elderly man in a seersucker suit. His face was lined, his hair snowy, his nose narrow and his eyes a surprising green highlighted with sparks of silver.

Exactly like Hollis's eyes.

She kept her gaze on the man as the maître d' helped her into an oversize leather chair. She hadn't yet met her father, but she knew this man was kin. The resemblance between him and herself unnerved her.

He seemed as stricken by her appearance as she was by his. Maybe he was simply shocked by her attire, but his gaze remained on her face even as Ray introduced himself and sat down next to Hollis.

"Who are you?" the old man asked her.

"My name is Hollis Griffin. I'm Olivier DuChesne's daughter." She was startled at how easy it was to say those words—and how much it hurt to say them.

Henri Marais cupped his hands around the glass before him. "I've already gotten myself a bourbon," he told Ray. "I reckon perhaps you might require a drink, too."

Ray ordered brandy for Hollis and a beer for himself. Just like their first meeting, she recalled, a meeting during which she was as overwhelmed as Henri Marais seemed to be now.

"I was born out of wedlock. Olivier DuChesne refused to acknowledge me," she went on, wondering whether Ray was going to interrupt and take over. She was glad he didn't. Obviously he realized that, despite her weakened physical state, she was strong enough to speak for herself. "My mother was Moira Hollis. She was a waitress. She loved Olivier DuChesne very much, even though he didn't love her. She named me Annabelle, after—"

"My sister," murmured Henri Marais. "Annabelle was my sister." He sipped his bourbon, and when he lowered the glass, a faint smile tinged his lips. "Dear, dear, my nephew has lived a messy life. But I never expected such a blessing to come from it."

"A blessing?" Perplexed, Hollis turned to Ray. His expression remained neutral as he observed the elderly man across the linen-covered table. She turned back to Henri Marais, too. "I'm your nephew's unclaimed, unnamed, illegitimate daughter. How is this a blessing?"

"Every child is a blessing," he said serenely. "What brought you to New Orleans?"

"Mr. DuChesne hired Ray to find me," Hollis continued when Ray said nothing. "He wanted to meet me."

"Yes, of course. He's dying. I reckon he wants the ledger clear before he passes on."

"That's what I thought, too." She was tired of talking, and unsure she was handling the conversation correctly. She wished Ray would jump in, but he only sat in the deep, high-backed leather chair, an impartial witness.

"How old are you?" Henri asked.

"Twenty-seven."

"Dear Lord. You know what this means, don't you?"

"It means I was born twenty-seven years ago."

"It means," he explained, "that you're Olivier's oldest surviving child."

The waiter arrived with her brandy. She raised the snifter to her lips and sipped as she contemplated his statement.

Henri leaned forward, speaking directly to her. His eyes were bright, his entire face alive with excitement. "It means that when Olivier dies you will inherit Serault Manor."

She choked on a mouthful of brandy. "What?"

"Serault Manor carries a legacy. The oldest surviving child must inherit the estate. If anyone breaks the legacy, a curse befalls the entire family.

She laughed at the sheer absurdity of it. A curse? Sure, she might have just been brought back from the dead by Nanny Carre's voodoo potions and chants, but a *curse?*

Like the curse Ray believed in, the curse that would visit any woman he was close to because he had inadvertently brought death upon his wife.

"You people are insane," she said, feeling uncomfortable when no one joined her laughter. "Curses like that don't exist."

"Oh, yes, they do," Henri corrected her. "Someone once broke the legacy, and the family was nigh wiped out. No one has broken it since. As long as you're alive when Olivier dies, Serault Manor is yours."

"That's why he tried to kill you," Ray said quietly.

Again she nearly choked, although this time she wasn't in the midst of drinking. It was her own despair she was choking on. "You think he tried to kill me so I wouldn't inherit his house?"

"What-all is this you're saying?" Henri interjected. "My nephew tried to kill you?"

"He poisoned her," Ray informed Henri, no trace of emotion in his voice. "I was able to get her away before the poison finished her off. She was close to death, though. I was nearly too late."

"Because he wanted the twins to get the house," Henri surmised, shaking his head furiously. "He had even tried to tamper with the legacy so his son would inherit. The only way he could keep the estate in the DuChesne family would be to make sure you weren't the oldest surviving child." Henri muttered something under his breath. "Dear child, what a terrible thing has been done to you. Olivier has lived a profligate life, and now that he's dying he must figure it's too late to change. I'm sure he wanted only to protect the twins. How dreadful that he should try to sacrifice you to keep the estate in his family." He shook his head in dismay. Then a dawning smile captured his face. "But you *are* family, Miss Griffin. You *are* a

Serault. A Marais. A DuChesne. You are one of us, and I shall see to it that the manor goes to you."

"I don't want it," she said quickly.

Henri looked affronted. "What do you mean, you don't want it? It is the grandest house in New Orleans. In all of Louisiana, if the truth be told. It is the pride of our family. You *must* inherit it."

The man was a lunatic. She didn't believe in his family's legacy or its ridiculous curse. If Ray didn't love her, there was no way in hell she was going to keep a house in New Orleans. "I don't want it. I live in upstate New York."

"But when Olivier dies you shall live in Serault Manor."

"I will not. If I have to inherit the house, I'll just sell it. I could sell it to the twins, and—"

"Oh, no, no, no. Dear girl, you must understand. If you sell it, the twins will be doomed. For their sake, and the sake of their children and all the generations to come, you must accept Serault Manor and live in it. They themselves would insist on this, for the sake of their children and posterity. You *must* make Serault Manor your home."

"I can't live in New Orleans." She turned in her chair and found Ray gazing at her. His eyes were dark, rueful, haunted. "Ray can tell you why," she murmured, then pushed out her chair and hobbled away from the table in Evaline's too-big shoes.

Ray caught up with her outside the front door, under the broad awning. "Hollis." He gripped her arm, holding her in place. "Don't run away."

"Why the hell shouldn't I run away? I don't want to live here in this crazy city where people try to kill each other because of some goofy superstition—or they're afraid to love each other because of some irrational fear—"

"Hollis." He held her other arm, forcing her to look at him. His face was contorted with pain, with regret. "It's not irrational. It's my life. I lived it, Hollis. I lived through the agony of watching a woman I loved die because of me. And I came too close to reliving that agony last night. I brought you to Olivier DuChesne and you almost died. It was my fault, Hollis. *My fault.*"

What she saw when she gazed up into his face was love. Desperate, frightening love. "You do love me." She didn't ask. She simply stated the truth.

"I don't want to. I can't. I'm afraid of what might happen to you."

"What might happen already did happen," she reminded him. "And you saved my life."

He pulled her to himself and crushed her lips with his. She sensed hope in his kiss, and hopelessness. When he pulled back, his eyes were even darker, shadowed with grief. "I couldn't bear it if I lost you."

"If I leave, we'll both be lost. You're my life, Ray."

"Then stay." It was a command, a plea. It was surrender.

"I'll stay." She slipped her hands around his neck and pulled him down for a kiss. "Can't curses be broken?"

"I hope so." He kissed her again, gently this time, and closed his arms around her. "Because you're my life, too. And I don't want to be lost again."

Their kiss was long and deep and hot. Ray's arms bound her to him, his body held her, his love enveloped her. If the doorman hadn't come over and tapped Ray's shoulder, the kiss might never have ended.

"Excuse me, sir," the doorman drawled, "but Monsieur Marais would like to know if he can expect your return."

Ray loosened his embrace only the slightest bit. "We're coming back in," he told the doorman. "I believe we've got some plans to make regarding Ms. Griffin's impending move to New Orleans."

"Yes," said Hollis, taking Ray's arm and leaning against him—not from weakness but from strength, and love. "I think it's time for me to come home."

Epilogue

Ray glanced up from the hammock as Hollis climbed onto the porch. She'd been down by the water's edge, photographing Spanish moss. According to Suzanne, her dealer back in New York, the recent show of Mississippi flora was selling phenomenally well.

"There's still a demand for mushrooms, though," Suzanne had said.

Hollis refused to shoot mushrooms anymore. "I don't like them," she had told Suzanne. "I know they're beautiful, but they're deadly. I intend to stick with the wildlife of the delta for a while."

She loved the batture, maybe even more than Ray did. The gardens around Serault Manor, where they spent their weekdays, were too manicured—lovely to look at, Hollis explained, but much too tame. She only liked to capture nature in the wild with her camera.

Being able to return to her photography had given her a much-needed route to tranquility after the tumult of her return to the DuChesne family fold. Her first years in town had been filled with unpleasant publicity: arrests, charges of attempted murder, the shock and distress Lenore DuChesne and her two children had undergone when they'd discovered the sort of man Olivier was.

He'd died before his case went to trial—in his own bed, since he'd been free on bail. Lenore and the twins had moved out of Serault Manor during those last few months. Hollis had lived with Ray. An army of nurses—total strangers—had ushered Olivier out of the living world. Minnie and Lowery had been unable to attend him, having been tried, convicted as accessories to attempted murder and sentenced to prison.

For a long time after the sensational trial, Lenore had refused to have anything to do with Hollis. The twins, however, accepted her. They understood that none of what had happened was her fault, and they believed, as their superstitious father and great-uncle and all the generations before them had, that her willingness to take title to the estate guaranteed their own health and prosperity.

Ollie, her half brother, had helped her and Ray to create a studio in the basement of the mansion, tucked between the wine cellar and the laundry room. She'd set up her enlarger and her darkroom equipment, and she spent many happy hours in the cool, stone cellar, developing the nature prints that Suzanne had no trouble selling for outrageous sums of money in New York.

Once the studio was complete, Ollie had moved out, heading to Atlanta for law school. "Only way I can live down my daddy's treachery is to fight for the law," he'd resolved.

"Yes," Hollis had agreed. "Plus, given all his convoluted business dealings, a law degree will help you figure out how to manage the family wealth."

"You can manage your own wealth," he'd argued.

Hollis had shaken her head. "If you won't manage my share of the fortune because you're my brother, then I'll damned well hire you to do it. What'll it be?"

"Hell, if I've got to manage that much money, maybe I'd better go to business school, too," Ollie had grumbled.

Ray liked Ollie. For a man who ought to have been spoiled by his uncommon wealth and privilege, he'd turned out a decent fellow with an earthy sense of humor. Hollis liked Ollie, too, but Claire was really a sister to her. They even bore a vague resemblance to each other, with their porcelain skin and dark hair and a shared love of plant life. Claire oversaw the garden maintenance at Serault Manor, and when Hollis balked at hiring a new staff to run the estate, Claire volunteered to take care of that, as well.

"I've never had help in my life—not *that* kind of help," Hollis had fretted.

"Don't y'all worry your head about that," Claire had assured her. "I'll handle the help. You handle Mother."

It took Lenore two years to come around. Two years of Henri Marais making pleas, two years of Hollis sending her letters and flowers and invitations and, finally, storming the elegant apartment Lenore had moved into overlooking Lake Pontchartrain. "I could use a mother," Hollis had said, "and you're all I've got. I want a family."

"Why not tell that detective of yours to give you one?" Lenore had shot back, as feisty as Hollis.

"I want a mother, damn it. And I want her to live at Serault Manor."

Eventually, that was exactly what Lenore did. She still oversaw half the charities in town, still bedecked herself with jewels and occasionally took to discussing Claire's suitors with Hollis.

"I wouldn't care to have her marry a detective," she'd remarked one recent afternoon as they sipped tea in the solarium. "But you've made such a fine marriage for yourself—a better marriage than mine, I'm afraid. I want Claire to find someone who's as perfect for her as Ray is for you."

Hollis had shared this discussion with Ray later that night. "And what advice did you give her?" he asked, pulling his beautiful wife into his arms and drawing the summer quilt over their bodies.

"I told her Claire should marry someone who's talented in the sack," Hollis said with a grin that quickly transformed into a rapturous sigh as Ray demonstrated a few of his many talents.

Those talents had left Hollis in an awkward state. Ray continued to watch from the porch hammock as she hauled her beautifully ungainly body up the steps, set her camera down on a table and sank wearily into the old cane-back rocker. He would have assisted her, but he knew she'd give him bloody hell if he did.

"I don't think you should be tramping around the levee in your condition," Ray couldn't help scolding.

"Oh, stop. I'm in excellent condition."

"Excellent for a woman who's less than two months from bringing forth the next heir of Serault Manor." He leaned forward, grabbed her hands and hauled her out of the rocking chair. She tumbled forward onto the hammock, just as he'd planned. "You're getting so big," he murmured, adjusting himself to make room for her on the soft netting. "And here I always used to think I preferred slim women to fleshy ones."

"It's your fault I look like a blimp."

"You don't look like a blimp," he murmured, raising himself gingerly so he wouldn't overturn the hammock. Hollis nestled into the fabric next to him. Smiling, he dropped a light kiss on her lips. "You look gorgeous. And I'll gladly take the credit for it." He ran his hands over her newly heavy breasts, then down to her swollen belly. He held her, wondering whether the baby inside could feel its daddy's embrace. "Have I thanked you today for saving my life?" he asked.

She smiled up at him. In her eyes he saw the green of the forest and the river and everything alive on earth. In her full, sweet lips and her delicate cheeks and her smooth, pale skin he saw everything he wanted, everything he needed. Everything he'd come so close to losing.

She used to argue with him when he said she'd saved his life. "No," she would protest, "*you* saved *mine*," and they'd get into a silly fight about who'd saved whom.

But finally he'd convinced her. She had broken the curse of his guilt. She had rid him of his fear of losing someone he loved. She had rescued him as surely as he'd rescued her.

"You've only thanked me once today," she told him.

"Well, then, I reckon I'd better thank you again," he murmured, bowing and kissing her more deeply.

In the heat of a sultry delta afternoon, with the river gliding past the batture and the trees shielding them from their neighbors and the sun, Ray and Hollis rejoiced in the glory of being saved. Alive. Together.